THE FORK RIVER SPACE PROJECT

BOOKS BY WRIGHT MORRIS

THE FORK RIVER SPACE PROJECT

A novel by

Wright Morris

HARPER & ROW, PUBLISHERS
New York, Hagerstown, San Francisco, London

For JO

FIRST EDITION

Designed by Gloria Adelson

ISBN: 0–06–013014–8
Library of Congress Catalog Number: 77–3798

77 78 79 80 10 9 8 7 6 5 4 3 2 1

I

I HAVE JUST DISCOVERED I can magnify objects by a slight pressure on the lids of my eyes. My head lies on the pillow, a fold of the bedspread touches my nose. The weave is coarse. If I press lightly on the lids of my eyelids the material of the spread looks like a fishnet. If I lid my eyes and turn to face the light, I see a color glowing like heated metal. Across it motes flick, like water insects. The color changes to a smog-filtered sunset. If I give myself over to this impression, I am free-falling in space (that is my sensation), and only by an effort do I recover my bearings. I owe this to Harry Lorbeer. He started me thinking—or should I say seeing? On the mind's eye, or on the balls of the eyes, or wherever it is we see what we imagine, or imagine what we see.

If you browse in magazines sold on supermarket counters you may have remarked the name Serenus Vogel. That is my pen name. I do humorous, fantasy-type pieces. Prior to my meeting with Harry Lorbeer I did not take people seriously. In the checkout line at the market this morning the clerk said to me, "Could you recommend an agent?" He had seen my face on a book jacket. I confess I was slow to make the connection. "I've got this story," he went on, "about my father. I need help with the Cuban background." This young man is tall, sandy-haired, and free of what I would describe as Cuban characteristics. His name is Carl. I read it on the name tag that said he was eager to serve me. People do have their place if we can just determine what it is.

Prior to my meeting with Harry Lorbeer I was researching a piece of an historical nature. Not far from our house wagon tracks wind across a field in a westerly direction, but you can't perceive them at ground level. They turn up in aerial photographs made in a government survey during the depression. You have to know what you're seeing. The pressure on the eyeball must be just right.

I have a fire-blackened penny, dated 1851, found in an ashpit with human bones, two sardine tins, musket balls, and arrowheads. Would you say that is history or science fiction? My wife and I live on the eastern rim of the plains, near the southerly fringe of the last great ice sheet. From the air you can see where the ice scoured the surface, rolling up balls of turf from the ancient sea's bottom. Some are petrified. My friend Rainey refers to them as dinosaur turds. Eleven miles due west a man-made mini-crater seats sixty thousand rabid football fans in season. They wear red hats and jackets and in a period of excitement might suggest that the crater is in eruption. What you see out here is from where you see it, and what you know. I see wagon tracks, covered wagons, hounded Indians, horse thieves, fur trappers, and plagues of grasshoppers. My neighbor on the south sees only the weather. His eyes are faded and creased from sky gazing. His wife's people see corn, soybeans, and beef cattle, with the exception of her brother, an engineer, who sees freeways. I have an uncle who is big in center pivot irrigation. He flies an airplane and takes his own pictures. From a few miles in space the pivot system leaves a pattern of circles like a target. An orbiting satellite might read them as a warning, or as a welcome. My friend Rainey, the weather man, sees prehistoric creatures waddling in a vast inland sea. He prefers what he sees to the missile silos that are actually there. My wife, Alice, sees the frost that will kill her garden. On my way to the market I often note a woman gazing over the half curtain at her kitchen window. Before her, westward, roll the endless plains, but it is not what she sees. It could be

3

that this is the right place for her, as it is for me. I sit here for hours with my fire-blackened penny, my fingers resting on my eyelids. In the blackness of space I see a cloud-wreathed object with jade green seas, smooth as marble, splattered with sable-colored islands. Here and there patches of land, like wrinkled skin, or sweeps of sand fine as talcum, but no sign of life, or death for that matter.

Am I a member of the first landing party? Knowing what I know, dare I risk it? The continents corrupted, the seas polluted, every living thing converted into pet food? I wake up with dry lips, filmed with perspiration. To get back to where I sit I need a decompression chamber. And there's the crux of the matter—at least according to Harry. Why should we come back? There's a knack to it, of course, and you'd better believe it. I am now in touch with people who are working on it. In one of the recent movies I've seen primates huddled in terror at a cave's mouth. What I seem to see is a single, many-eyed monster, paralyzed with fear. The primates look alike, but that's misleading. One of them has the idea he is *human.* Just an idea, no way to prove it. What he had to be was crazy enough to believe it. In no time at all, historically speaking, he had the whole tribe of apes believing as he did, covering the walls of their caves with pictures. It's contagious. Nobody knows where such an idea will lead to. Nor am I sure Harry Lorbeer has given it much thought.

It occurs to me that I have never heard Harry raise his voice. He is calm. He looks at me as he would a wayward child. Harry is short, getting a little paunchy, with a somewhat vacant, disinterested manner. Uncertain that I'm getting his full attention, I raise my voice. He has asked Alice if I'm hard of hearing. He brings along with him, when he works, a pair of the blue overalls worn by farmers, with the shoulder straps, the bib, and the whine when his thighs rub. He often wears a white carpenter's apron to carry his tools. He uses a hippie-type van to dress in, and sits in the cab to eat his lunch from a paper bag. It's my business to note these little details. If there's going to be a change, people like Harry will make it. All he needs, as I see it, is someone to believe in him. He already has Dahlberg. If I am any judge of the matter, he's getting to me.

Harry Lorbeer is not the sort of person who would catch your eye in the street. I am. Just yesterday morning, picking up the laundry, which I carry in a candy-striped bag with a noose, I was stopped by a stranger who asked me if I cut my own hair. It just so happens I do. I've cut it since the price went up in the sixties. I also live in a community where people feel free to ask their neighbors pertinent questions. My point is, he asked *me,* and he wouldn't have asked Harry. To that extent, at least, I stand out from the crowd. Without his carpenter's apron Harry wouldn't. Alice also tells me he is slow to blink his eyes.

Four or five weeks ago—it seems longer—I called the local hardware for the name of a handyman or a plumber. We've got a plumber, but he can no longer afford to work for us. For a small-time job, say opening a sink drain, he has to come on the weekend and charge me overtime. It hurts him to do that. On my time we've discussed it at length. The hardware people recommended Harry Lorbeer, and when I called I got an answering service. Three or four days later he called me back.

"What's your problem?" he asked me. I explained we had a clogged drain in the bathroom washbowl. "Tell your wife not to wash her hair in it," he said. I explained that Alice washed her hair in the tub, and took every possible precaution. "Take a wire coat hanger, mister, untwist it at the neck until you got one long wire, then crook a hook on one end of it and stick it down the drain, fish for the hair with it." I explained that I doubted it was hair, since I'm the one who uses the bowl and I've little hair to lose. "I'm twenty-eight miles southeast," he said, "and you'd like me to drive fifty-six miles to fish a little hair out of your drain?"

Thinking fast I said, "We've got a deck that needs painting. Do you paint?"

"I don't paint," he replied. "Dahlberg paints."

"I've had a union estimate," I said. "I'd appreciate a non-union estimate."

"He gets three dollars an hour. You supply the paint."

That was so good I didn't believe it. "Where you people located?" I said.

He replied, "Heber County. We're in Kansas." Heber County is south of the east-west freeway, and people who live in the north see little of it. I assumed they were farmers who did odd jobs on the side. "What I'll do," he went on, "I'll stop by when I'm in the neighborhood, right?"

Before I could say yes or no, he hung up. During the week or ten days we didn't hear from him I took a wire coat hanger, untwisted it the way he said, hooked a crook on the end, and fished around in the bowl drain. What I came up with you wouldn't believe. I refused to let Alice see it. Gobs of sludge with the density of axle grease skillfuly blended with wadded bits of Kleenex. Alice uses bits of tissue to wipe out the bowl. I hauled out a cup of it. I called Alice in to watch the water running and make a few tactful suggestions about tissues. The banging on the door startled us both. Not familiar with a man who said his name was Harry my wife delayed opening the door for him. I ran down the bathroom window to check on him. Two men were at the door.

"I'm Harry Lorbeer," said the short one, "this is Dahlberg."

Lorbeer had left his car in the street, and walked in with his box of plumber's tools. He wore his overalls and his carpenter's apron. I thought he looked pale and sallow for a farmer. The fellow with him was tall, his hair clipped so short I could see his scrubbed suntanned scalp. Copper-colored wiry hairs glistened on his forearms, the backs of his hands. Alice would have said he looked squeaky clean.

After I opened the door I had the problem of explaining that I had taken his advice, about the coat hanger, and just that moment had opened the drain. Harry seemed pleased. "Watch the hair," he said, glancing at mine, and checked two of the faucets for drips. "While I'm here," he said, "I'll change the washers."

"Great!" I said.

"Show him your deck," he said to me, and I walked ahead of Dahlberg to the door to the deck, off the living room. He walked out on it as if he doubted it would hold his weight. He had the gangly spread-legged walk you see in stiff-jointed old men. From the back his head was knobby, the flesh of his neck lumpy and pockmarked. He showed less interest in the deck than the view we've got, and Alice's garden.

"Nice place," he said. He was one of these big fellows with a small, high-pitched voice.

"We like it," I said, "but it's a lot of work."

He used his nail to fleck scaling paint off the deck rail.

"I see the trim's the same color, want me to paint the trim?"

"I would," I said, "if you can find the time."

"You don't find time, Mr. Kelcey, you make it. If you'd like me to make the time, I'll do it." He talked looking away, squinting at our view, as if he was forcing the words through his teeth.

"When can you make it?"

In the door at my back Harry Lorbeer said, "That's what we don't know. We go from day to day."

I wondered what he meant to be saying. Either his humor was so dry I didn't catch it, or I failed to follow his thinking. He looked at me without blinking, his lips puckered as if he might whistle.

"Don't you find people need to know when to expect you?"

"Not us," he said, "it can't be helped. We might be here and we might be in orbit."

Had I heard him correctly? His expression had not changed. Dahlberg stood with his back to me.

In my boyhood I heard stories of how the smell of the paint made boozers out of house painters. I thought it highly likely. "What do we do," I said, "just wait for you to turn up?"

"We're all just waiting," said Harry, "isn't that right?"

It's been my experience that the really funny people are those you just stumble on, like Harry. He had the role down pat. As Alice later remarked, his eyes were slow to blink.

"Well," I said, "if it's the deck, it hardly matters. You can work on it whether we're here or not."

Harry nodded. He and Dahlberg had a way of passing signals that only comes with years of living together. They both left the deck and walked back through the house to where Harry had left his tool box. Harry was bald on the top, but he let his hair grow long at the back. I was thinking what an odd couple they made, but how well they had worked out their own problems. Back in some farmhouse, out of sight and off the highway, they uncorked the bottle and went into orbit.

"Let me pay you for the plumbing work," I said.

Harry said, "Twenty-four dollars plus parts."

"For washers? That's as much as my plumber."

"I *am* your plumber. Good plumbers aren't cheap."

Alice runs the finances in our family. She wrote him out a check. "Before we go on," I said, "let's have a clear understanding. How much are you charging me to paint the deck?"

Harry said, "Three dollars an hour, plus the paint."

"Two days is about fifty dollars," I said, "not including the paint." They both nodded. "How come one of you works for three dollars an hour, and the other one for forty bucks an hour?"

"A good plumber is not cheap," Harry repeated.

There was no point in my arguing about it if I ever hoped to get the deck painted. "What town you people live near?"

"We live in Fork River," said Dahlberg, "we don't live near it."

Harry puckered his lips, but said nothing.

"I don't think I know it," I said.

They did not say that I should.

"Well, I hope you can make it soon," I said, and followed them down the drive for a look at their car. They had a hippie-type van, with a Kansas license, the hood and sides ornamented with blue and yellow flower paintings. "Fork River's in Kansas?"

"Was when we left," said Dahlberg, which I took to be up-to-date Kansas humor.

On the top of the van were two paint-splattered metal ladders. Dahlberg took the wheel. While I stood watching them drive off he either didn't shift to high, or the car didn't have one.

"I'd just as soon not see *that* pair again," I said

to Alice, but Dahlberg was back the following morning, before we got up. I could hear the van groaning up the street, and the rattle of the ladders when he turned in the driveway. It hardly seemed to matter whether we were home or not. He managed to find the outside socket that I had always looked for, and plugged in his sander. That just about took care of my morning's work, but he had parked so I couldn't back out of the garage. When the sanding stopped I could hear the country music on the transistor radio in one of his coveralls pockets. He did not appear to loaf. I clocked him in less than thirty minutes for lunch, including two beers and a chat with Alice about the trellis she wanted him to build for her tomatoes. At four o'clock he quit, cleaned his brushes, and took off. I was ready for him the following morning, early, but he didn't show up.

2

"YOUR MOTHER AND I have our expectations," my father often said, whenever he wanted to express their concern for me. I'm not sure it is possible to say more than that, in so few words. Their expectations were that I would amount to something, which is both explicit and hard to define.

Since I was not in the best frame of mind for work, I took the morning off. I drove out the freeway, about twelve miles east, to Ansel Burger's gas station. The east-west freeway bisects the county and cuts Burger off from about half of his clients. His loyal customers have to drive six miles west to cross it, and those not so loyal buy their gas elsewhere. Burger has plenty of time to think, and he saves up his thoughts for his loyal customers. From the freeway I can see the colorful display of patchwork quilts his wife makes, and hopes to sell to the tourists. The next freeway exit, if they decide to buy a quilt, is eleven miles east. Burger will check the oil, if I ask him, or smear the windshield with a wad of newspaper. If I say, "Fill it up!" he always double-checks to see if I mean it. In the old days a dollar's worth of gas would last several weeks.

"How do I get to Fork River?" I asked him.

Burger has a squint that almost closes his eyes. He wears a brakeman's hat of blue and white denim, with a high squashed crown. He squinted into the glare of the sun. "How would I know that?"

"I think it's just across the line, in Kansas."

"You're asking me about Kansas?"

"Have you got a map?"

"It wouldn't be on it. The maps don't show anything with less than forty people."

You have to remember, as I do, that Burger is often lacking for conversation. I thanked him, and bought two of the pumpkins he had stacked in a pyramid between his gas pumps, a bit of local color for Alice. He took pride in saying, he said in closing, that he did not take credit cards, and passed mine back to me.

Ten miles to the south I made another stop, where I was shown a map with the Fork River on it, but no town. If it had been on the map, I might have looked no further for it. As it was, I stopped off to see Miss Ingalls, the local librarian. She dates from a time when writers were important people, and wears the paisley shawls that once draped grand pianos. She comes alive if I ask her questions. So many books that are useless prove to be useful. In one of them she found it: Fork River, a town in Kansas. In 1940 it had numbered more than seven hundred people. Where had those people gone?

Miss Ingalls assured me that it was not at all unusual, during the depression, for both the town and its people to disappear.

Not all of them, I said. I had met two of them. Harry Lorbeer, a plumber, and his friend Dahlberg.

"Dahlberg?" she echoed.

"He's the painter. He's doing some work for us."

Miss Ingalls had turned to the card file at her back. She took out one of the drawers, flicked through the cards.

"Dahlberg, O. P.," she read aloud. *"A Hole in Space and Other Stories.* I just knew we had a Dahlberg."

"He writes?"

"He once did. It's 1962."

Should I read the fiction of our new deck painter? "Is there something by Lorbeer, Harry?" I inquired. Plumbers would not be lacking in raw material. There were several Lorbeers, but no Harry. I could see that the prospect aroused Miss Ingalls; she visibly nibbled the bait.

"Why don't I check on the Dahlberg," she said. In a moment she was back with a well-thumbed paperback, a picture of the author on the glossy jacket. He had not changed. He stood with his fingers poised at his hips, as if his stance had been determined by calculation. In his pose there was longing, hankering, and contempt.

"That's him," I said.

"Born in Provo, Utah," Miss Ingalls read from the jacket, "of a Swedish immigrant father and a Mormon mother."

"That makes for a hole in something," I said. "I'll take it." Miss Ingalls was pleased.

"I just knew I'd heard of a Dahlberg," she said, which I thought would be a nice thing to tell him. Nothing equals being heard of, to an author. But the moment I saw his van parked in the drive, where I couldn't get around it, I thought better of it. He was at work on the deck.

"I see you made it," I said.

"I had to drop Harry off in Seward," he replied. Seward is about twenty miles to the west. I didn't think it was the time to mention the book to Alice, so I went back to my study to read it. The opening story was titled *The Taste of Blood*. It concerned a youth who lived in Provo, Utah, the only child of

16

Mormon parents. His mother took in washing to support his invalid father. That doesn't sound very encouraging, but you have to let him tell it.

Would his life have been different if he had let his hair grow? On his hands and chest, where one saw more of it, it was honey-colored with a golden glisten, like that on a singed chicken. His whining high-pitched voice was made for country music, his smile like a string of pearls in his pockmarked face. Along with this, his muffled sizzling laugh was like the sound of a fuse burning. An inch taller than Lincoln, some found him ugly enough to be handsome. Of all the Mormons in Provo, what had led him to think he should write? Quite by accident he had stumbled on *The Grapes of Wrath*. He liked the turtle. He couldn't get the turtle out of his mind. Actually he didn't get much beyond the turtle, but that was far enough to do the damage.

That's on page two, and by page five he has left Provo, Utah, for a religious school in Walla Walla, Washington. Uninstructed in the school's religious doctrine, he was puzzled by the prevailing customs. There was a large gymnasium, but it sat empty. The students seemed to be ignorant of basketball, football, and such sports. Being a good basketball player, thanks to his height, he persuaded students in his dormitory to come out and "shoot baskets" with him. After a little of that, he had them choosing up sides, playing games. Not one of them breathed a word to him that "competitive" sports were forbidden. They almost went crazy with excitement. Nothing like this had ever happened to them. They played barefoot, not having the shoes they needed, and tore their clothes pretty badly in the heated scuffles. It amused the young man to see these grown young men scuffling like kids. They pushed, shoved, tore each other's clothes, but it didn't cross their minds to take offense, and get into a fight. One afternoon three of the boys were scrapping for the ball and Dahlberg moved in to try to separate them. He got an elbow in the mouth that cut his lip and loosened one of this teeth. This put him in such a rage he began to swing blindly, and they all began to fight like a pack of animals. By the time it was stopped all of the boys were bloody, and the teacher who had intervened had an injured eye, his shirt torn off his back. A taste of blood was all that was needed to turn decent young men into wild animals. Naturally, Dahlberg was asked to leave, but he had been too ashamed to go back to Provo. He became a sort of tramp, hitching rides on the highway, working at odd jobs for his meals. He worked in a logging camp in California. It gave him all the time in the world to think. He came to the conclusion that competition, not money, was the root of most evil. Men were passive enough to begin with, but they learned to be brutes. Wherever competition was encouraged, the only goal in life was winning. The ultimate winner was a killer. The ultimate contest was war. When he had thought it all out he sat down and wrote his story, *The Taste of Blood,* which won a prize of fifty dollars in a short story contest. That made him a winner. Otherwise nothing in the world had changed.

The idea behind the story was not so unusual, but I must say I liked the way Dahlberg told it. For the first few minutes after I read it I really *believed* it, the way he did. If the goddam competition would stop, wouldn't we all be better for it? The ultimate winner *is* a killer, and the ultimate killer *is* war. But a lot of men know that. Not a one of them has been able to do more than round up a few women, or give up eating meat and start drinking Postum. Sooner or later some barbarian will give them all the taste of blood.

I glanced up to see Dahlberg, right below my window, pulling off the green coveralls he wears when he paints. They fit him tight at the ankles and cuffs, and have chest-high zipper pockets. He was awkward as a gangly kid trying to put on a turtleneck sweater. It made him flustered. I could hear him muttering to himself. But what a different picture you get of a person when you catch a glimpse of what they are thinking. This dour, almost sullen, phlegmatic Swede, with his vision of a brotherhood of brutes. I felt warmly fraternal toward him. Cranking open my study window I said, "Will we see you tomorrow, Dahlberg?"

"Who knows?" he replied. Why do men with virtually no hair to comb dote on combing their hair? He raked the comb through his brush cut, then blew on the teeth, like a barber.

"It would help if we knew," I said. "We'd like to be able to make our plans—"

"Go ahead and make your plans. Just don't make me part of them."

That's the fellow who had just, almost, moved me to a gesture of fellowship. It was three o'clock. Why was he quitting so early? "I've got to pick up Harry in Seward," he said, reading my mind. I could have shattered his calm by just casually mentioning, "I've been reading a little story here," and waving it at him, "with the title of *The Taste of Blood*. I think you might find it of interest." I didn't of course. It would lose me my point of vantage. Once he was free of the coveralls he dusted them off, stuffed in the pockets, and hung them on a slope-shouldered wooden coat hanger. That's your experienced, neat-type bachelor, silent member of an odd couple. I would say he did the cooking. Harry swept up and made the beds.

"Well, have a nice day," I said, then shut the window. I walked through the house to where Alice stood at the door to the deck, checking his work. "At this rate," I said, "it will take him a week. Why don't I ever learn?"

"He's shy," she said. "He's so shy he blushes, his ears turn red."

"That could be his cooling system." She is now long accustomed to my type of humor. "Would you say he was bright?"

"What an odd question."

"Why is it odd?" I asked.

One of the things I admire about Alice is the way she never ruffles. It doesn't occur to her to take offense because our opinions differ. As she thinks her eyes dart around as if she might see the answer somewhere. "He's sweet," she said. "He is a very gentle person."

"Would you say he has talent?"

"As a house painter?"

"No, no, just talent. A gift for something or other."

"I think he's a person who might surprise you," she said, and closed the door to the deck.

"He has already. Miss Ingalls at the library tells me he's a writer."

That surprised her. "A poet?" Alice had come a bit early for the flower children, and would always feel she had missed something.

"Stories," I said, "some sort of science fiction."

"He's imaginative. When he smiles his homely face is simply radiant. I've never seen such white teeth."

"There's nothing like a pockmarked complexion to bring out the fine points," I said.

Alice has a sure sense of when a topic should be dropped. "I'm going to pick some fresh chard," she said, and slipped on her gardening gloves, with the green leather thumbs. She filled her watering can at the patio spigot and carefully overwatered the fuschias. With my study window open I could hear the water drip on the bricks. In my typewriter was a yellow sheet of paper with these lines across the top.

In my boyhood it was rumored that the center of this country was in a town just forty miles to the west. To have been born so close to the heart of this great nation often gave me cause for wonder.

What was the wonder? It seemed to have slipped my mind. From the morning Harry Lorbeer said to me, "Take a wire coat hanger, untwist it at the neck until you got a long wire, then crook a hook on one end and stick it down the drain and fish for the hair with it," I have been subject to distractions. This morning I drove out to chat with Ansel Burger. An hour ago I sat here reading one of Dahlberg's stories. I have the book here on my desk. *A Hole in Space and Other Stories*. The book has illustrations, black and white pen drawings, and one of them shows a wide stretch of the prairie with a small round hole, like an eye, in the overcast sky. Right beneath the hole a piece of the highway and part of a filling station, including sections of roadside motel cabins, have disappeared. Tiny ant-like figures stand peering up at the hole in the sky. That would be one of his sci-fi pieces, and I liked the way he got right down to business.

On a warm October day, of the sort that alerts weather watchers, a man from the state light and power people drove over to Fork River to turn off the lights. No payments had been received since the first of July. He found the school bus as usual, at the highway turnoff, but it had been stripped to a hulk. From the highway there was little to be seen of Fork River since it sat in the arroyo cut by the river.

It occurred to me, reading the story, that I was faced with something you don't see at eye level: you have to see it from space, like a mini-crater, or the tracks covered wagons had left crossing the plains. Oddly enough, the overview from space was more common to early man than it is to us. They were not limited to their own view. You can see that in the cave paintings, and the Easter Island sculptures. They are not propped up there for people to see, but for avenging gods. They look in the direction that gods might come from. The best example of this is Stonehenge. From the dwarfed level of man it's a scattered pile of rocks: you have to see it from space to get the message, and that's from where the gods see it. I'm not suggesting that an airview of Fork River will spell out a new and wondrous revelation, but I know that if I mentioned it to Harry or Dahlberg they would not be surprised.

3

THIS MORNING I told Alice that I would check with Miss Ingalls as to what books they had by Dahlberg. *The Taste of Blood* would shock and delight her, but I felt uneasy about *A Hole in Space*. Winds of any kind disturb her. Cyclones terrify her. She would rather be taken by surprise, she says, than cower waiting in a corner of the basement, if she could remember the right corner. She might not want to read about a piece of the earth, more than three acres of it, along with the highway, a gas station, several buildings, and an undetermined number of people, just whooshing off through a hole in the sky. It's implausible, of course. But would you say it was impossible? If some trickster neutralized a cone of gravity, like the column of a twister but without the disorder, the raging inferno around the vacuum, anything within the cone, not battened down, would zoom off into space like a rocket. Loose topsoil, houses, cars, cattle, and people, along with strips of highway dangling like Band-Aids. I can already see it as a movie. A cone like that, without gravity, might slurp up a good-sized body of water, as if sucked through a straw. We're accustomed to things disappearing. How about lakes? This seems pretty remarkable, if we're earthbound, and gaze upward to see it happening, but it's not an unusual event if seen from space. A tiny puff of debris, like seeds blown on the winds of space. My friend Rainey says the remarkable thing is not what disappears, but all that stays put. He says that any day now some smart alec will come up with a do-it-yourself anti-gravity kit. You just rub it on, like suntan oil, then paddle around in the air like a fish. It's not a new idea. The old masters filled their paintings with unidentified flying objects. What is it, he asks me, that man has imagined that hasn't come to pass?

The horseshoe bend in the Fork River, Miss Ingalls tells me, was once the location of Devil's Nest, a rendezvous point for fur traders, trappers, cattle rustlers, thieves, and desperadoes. What the frontiersman saw from the bluffs of the Missouri was the uneven floor of an extinct sea, but luckily he didn't know it. He might have thought twice about trying to cross it. Had the wagon trains and gold seekers known it, some would have surely turned back, their doomed lives saved. Not once, I guess, but many times the wall of ice advanced and receded. Between the seasons of ice dinosaurs waddled and huge bat-like birds, the size of gliders, flapped their wings in air thick enough to swim in. For someone with a dinosaur's point of view, it must have been a place of great expectations. In a twist of fortune that appeals to me, that is also how the early settlers saw it. Man and beast found it appealing, wet or dry. The one notable exception were the women. Could we say they saw it for what it was? Not a tree for shade. No place for either creatures or humans to hide. The one departure was the occasional river that cut ravines deep enough to camp in. The Fork River was one, the tops of the willows looking like bushes if seen from the plain. That's how one pioneer described it. I love the elevated, oratorical style that came natural to the writer.

As my mind reaches back to the long ago, and once familiar faces cluster round, my eye dwells upon the treeless plain that rolled and swelled like the open sea.

I doubt this fellow knew what the sea looked like, until he saw the great plains.

The reader must not expect these memories to be free [he writes] of an occasional dip into the vulgar, because I write of characters more uncouth than those we see in Heber County today.

That was dated 1887. He believed that uncouthness was about to be banished. I can be as distracted by a line like that as by the sepia photograph that goes along with it, showing the author, dressed for Sunday, on the buckboard seat of a wagon. The horse, the wagon, and the bearded writer now gone. All gone. I'm so affected by reports of that type of couthness that I pick up the writer's voice and manner. Alice has often remarked it. In something I am doing, or something I am saying, I'll slip in a passage that I appear to have received from a departed spirit, in a seance. Miss Ingalls, who may be ten years my senior, is so close in spirit to this past she has not actually departed from it. She is dry as a twig, and there's little juice in her, but she can crackle like a brush fire when her "dander's stirred up" as she says. She felt that Fork River, given my interest, might very well repay a visit, since some of these out-of-the-way little ghost towns were very well preserved in the dry climate.

Why had such a village, of more than seven hundred people, suddenly died off? Miss Ingalls said there was always information about things that were growing, towns that were rising, but it was usually lacking about places that were declining. There had been the depression, for one thing, and the surrounding dust bowl for another. It must have crossed one of their minds that the jig was up. A compact community, of one ethnic group, would share that opinion like a family. Once one of the respected members pulled up stakes, the rest would soon follow. If I was interested, Miss Ingalls suggested, why didn't I pay the town a visit and see for myself.

She also passed on to me a Xerox copy of a story called *Waiting*. The author's name is Bergdahl, but she doubts it. She feels the internal evidence is all for Dahlberg. It's the plain, unvarnished tale of a small town on its last legs. Most of the people have left or died. The others just sit around waiting. For what? For something to happen. They sit around on the porch of the general store looking at the sky, discussing the weather. Nothing happens. That would make a better title for the story up to that point than *Waiting*. But the waiting builds up. You get a wonderful sense of what is on their minds just from the way they don't talk about it, the way you get a sense of great expectations from people who say the least about it. It seemed to be a straightforward, realistic type of story, touching on an experience common to many people. Who wasn't *waiting?* Even the reader was waiting for the story to end. All of this was done so skillfully, so matter-of-factly, that when the UFO came skimming in like a Frisbee, and hovered over the square like a silent helicopter, I accepted it the way they did. Why not? Something had to happen. Why not something unusual? This big saucer just hovered—it didn't have to land, and made no more noise than a musical top—and through a green glow in its belly it sucked up the people who approached it. No hoodlum-type Martians, or beetle-legged space midgets, just this fairly commonplace but well-oiled flying saucer incorporating the improvements of the latest models. Not everybody left. The author didn't spell it out, but he seemed to imply that unless there was someone to go on *waiting*, there was no reason to assume things would go on happening.

On reflection I didn't mention this story to Alice, knowing what she would say.

In the morning Harry's van pulled up just after seven o'clock, turned in the drive, then took off. When I peered out the window I saw Dahlberg seated on the curb, reading our morning paper. He had his lunch in a bag, his coveralls in a roll bound up with a belt. He waited till about twenty minutes to eight, then he walked up the drive and around to the deck. I could hear him prying the lids off his cans, stirring up the paint. Like many painters I've observed he keeps a cigarette dangling from one corner of his mouth, but seldom puffs it. The smoke creases his eyes. When he looks up the ashes sprinkle his face. Down to the butt, he gives it a pinch, with his thumbnail, so the tobacco crumbles as he rolls the paper in a tight little wad. I have twice seen him flick it with his fingernail at the birds in the deck feedbox, just like a kid.

I'm not an early riser, but I cannot lie in bed while I pay someone to work. I made coffee, and walked to the deck door to ask Dahlberg if he would join me. If Alice had asked him he would have. "I don't hear your radio this morning," I said.

"I thought the missus might be sleeping," he replied.

This is what a woman means when she judges a hired hand as "sensitive."

"I see you don't have the van?"

"Harry has a job in Crete," he replied.

"You fellows don't lack work, I'll say that."

"If we want it," he replied, "we don't lack it."

"People don't mind this day-to-day, 'who knows what tomorrow will bring' business?"

"So long as we get the job done," he replied. Have you noticed the way a house painter has of thinning his brush against the lip of the can, first one side then the other? Dahlberg could do this in a way that had something subtly insolent about it, as if he took forever wiping his hands, while you stood and watched. On the other hand, I didn't feel that it was personal. He dispenses his insolence impartially. Alice would say that the way he dipped his brush, and thinned it on the can lip, was sensuous rather than insolent. I think that's true, and it might be why I felt its insolence.

Actually, I would like to have had a talk with Dahlberg about *A Hole in Space.* I don't read science fiction, if I can help it, and I wondered what his readers might have thought about it. Was it just a fantasy, or did some of them think it might have taken place? Dahlberg's touchy manner, as far as I was concerned, made it difficult for me to bring the matter up. He might think me nosy. He might think I was trying to "butter him up." I happened to be a writer myself but he showed no interest in what I might be. A more curious, observant person would wonder why I wasn't off somewhere, working. We've always had that trouble with housemaids. "What is it Mr. Kelcey *does?"* they ask Alice. Until they *know* what it is I do they are out of their minds. Dahlberg simply didn't seem to give a damn, which I find to be part of his normal stance. It's perfectly expressed in the way he stands, even with one hand holding a paintbrush. It's not so much a chip on his shoulder, as a chip that is all of one piece. My guess would be that he had had something more than just a taste of blood. I knew that if I asked him about Fork River he would clam up. Harry Lorbeer was a different type of person and would not think such a question personal, but Harry Lorbeer was a plumber spending the day in Crete. Why didn't I drive over and see for myself? Both Lorbeer and

Dahlberg would be away, and I could snoop around. As a rule I work in the morning, but in one way or another I found Dahlberg distracting. I can't stand country music. But it would be worse if I asked him to turn it off. I left a note for Alice that I had a few errands, and would be back for lunch.

I drove south ten miles, then east to Millard, which proved to be a few over twenty. At a station in Millard I asked how to get to Fork River, and the kid cleaning my windshield had never heard of it. "I'm new around here," he said, "but I'll ask Jake." Jake was down in one of the oil pits they used to have before they raised the cars on hoists. He walked back to where he could get a look at me, smears of grease on his bearded face. They talked for some time, while he rubbed at his hands with a rag. He wore a hat made out of the want ad section of a newspaper, folded so it was square, fit snug like a skullcap. Grease dripped on his ears and his face. The only concern he seemed to feel was for the top of his head. The kid came back and said did I know Fork River was a dead town? I said I knew that. How did I get there? He went back to Jake, who thought that over, then climbed out of the pit and walked to get a look at me.

"Howdy, mister," he said.

"Howdy," I said.

"What you want in Fork River?"

"I want to see if it's there," I said. That seemed

to stump him. He rubbed at his hands with the rag he was clutching.

"The road's closed," he said. "They got sawbucks up to close it. But there's room on the ditch side to drive around them."

"Where is this road?"

"You go four miles east. It's not much of a road."

"Why is it closed?"

"Costs money to keep it up."

"Nobody lives there?"

"How would I know that, mister?" He saw I was crazy. If I asked him one more question, and got one more answer, I would think so myself. I thanked him, and drove six or seven miles east before I realized I must have gone by it. Two miles back I found this turnoff overgrown with weeds, without a sign or road marker. Two battered sawbucks were in the ditch to one side, one with a sign stating ROAD CLOSED. The road was gravel, with weeds growing at the center, the tops lopped off about knee-cap high. In the ditch along the east side the sunflowers were coated with road dust. Just up ahead the road dipped into a gulley, and in the gulch on the right, twenty yards off the road, the battered hulk of a yellow school bus sat axle deep in the soft field loam. All the windows were shattered. The radiator and the seat frames were gone, the near side and the rear of the body had been riddled with bullet holes. A common enough road-side eyesore. Why did it seem familiar? It occurred to me that it resembled the bus Dahlberg had de-scribed in his story, given twenty years' time and looting. Less than a mile to the north, up a slow incline, the road crested on the horizon. What I took to be the dead branches of scrub bushes proved to be the tops of poplars and cottonwoods in the arroyo. They looked dead. Right at the sum-mit of the crest, without warning, the road jogged right and dropped steeply. The wrecked bodies of eight or ten cars were strewn about on the slope, where they had stopped rolling. The narrow one-way road was so gutted with runoffs the car scraped on the ridges, and I stopped to think it over. To get in and out of here one needed a jeep, or a van with high clearance. To the south and east the arroyo spread wide and I could see the distinct branches of the river, one bone dry, the other with a ripple at the center channel. Clumps of pale green willows grew thick on the islands. I had the curious impression of having stumbled on something lost. A flight of crows dipped to caw at me, then wing off to report their findings. I was less than ten miles off the free-way yet it seemed like another country. Hugging the cliff side of the road, where the ruts were shallow, I took it very slowly on the steep decline. On a curve I saw a park-like cluster of trees, and the first of several boarded-up frame houses. It was May, but most of the trees were leafless. The square buildings, once white, had the air of resort houses closed up for a season. They were not in bad shape. Heavy planks were nailed to the doors and the windows, and here and there I saw a porch swing drawn up to the ceiling, a once popular way to store them over the winter. What struck me was the absence of TV aerials. Not much remained of the lawns but sparse clumps of dead grass, the earth eroded and blown away from the roots. The houses had been patterned on the same simple design, with a porch at the front, a cellar door at the side, and either one or two gables, depending on the number of rooms. All these structures and trees were on the west side of the river, and got the morning sun. By four o'-clock—early in the winter—they would be in the shade of the arroyo wall. I was so taken with this park-like setting I stopped the car and looked at it. How the kids must have loved it. In the spring they had a river right there at their feet. The hard smoothness of the road indicated that in the rainy season the street was flooded. On up the ravine, where it narrowed, was probably what they referred to as Devil's Nest, a perfect hideout for thieves and cattle rustlers. Wondering where it was the natives had done their shopping I went along slowly, into a sudden clearing. The houses on my left were larger and closer together and faced the open area like a stage. Until that moment, because of the angle of the sun, I had not been able to see the solid row of structures, many with high false fronts, set up off the bed of the river on piers. My first impression was that the earth had been washed away beneath them. At the front a boardwalk, about waist high, ran the full length of the row to the steps at each end. The long deep shadow cast by these buildings seemed to open up a hole in the street. I had never seen a ghost town so compact and spare, so well preserved. It had the appearance of a movie set put together elsewhere, and brought in on flatcars and wagons. Everything perfect. No doors or windows broken. The pale shadow of letters on faded blinds and curtains. Under peeling paint I saw the ghostly name of a merchant, the date 1892. Backed up to the south end of the boardwalk were two railroad coaches the dusty color of Confederate uniforms. The coach blinds were drawn, as if the passengers were asleep. At nine thirty in the morning I couldn't say that what I felt was an eerie, unearthly feeling, but insofar as the time of day would allow I had never experienced an emotion quite like it. A lost world? But nothing had been lost. Less than seven miles away was the town of Millard, and three crowded supermarkets. The block of stores were of a single piece, but a wide variety of fading colors. All the false fronts tilted rearward, as if they had felt the pressure of the afternoon sun. A barber pole, surmounted by an eagle, stood to the left of a door that set in slantwise to the barber shop. Several curling posters leaned on the window, hung with the usual half curtain. In the spring water rippled and splashed under the boardwalk, but I found it hard to imagine. What had it been like? A lake village, hovering over the water, or a frontier-type Noah's ark? How explain that the country hoodlums, the souvenir collectors, hadn't ransacked it? I had forgotten that I knew two people who lived here. Were there others? No dogs barked. In lonely places of this sort people usually kept dogs. At the north end of the street, where the ravine narrowed, a school or meeting hall, with a peaked roof and a cupola at the front, with a bell, faced the open square. In the shaded yard at the side were swings, a teeter-totter, and wooden benches. The roof of the building had been repaired with sheets of galvanized metal, glinting like mirrors. I left my car and walked toward the school, the cupola crowded with cooing pigeons. A trash barrel at one side of the street was stuffed with frozen food cartons and supermarket bags. The ground was higher here, with enough topsoil to get rutted and muddy in the rainy season. A car, or cars, someone coming and going, had chewed up a large piece of it. I thought I caught a whiff, when the breeze stirred, of the pungent smell of manure and fodder. But there were no barns. A woodpecker hammered high in

one of the trees. From the steps to the school, re-
cently painted, I could see a small card pinned to
the door. It read

FORK RIVER SPACE PROJECT
Harry Lorbeer, Prop.
OPEN 2-5 Sat. & Sundays

The heavy doors had been bolted from the inside
—I could see a plank at waist level—with a slit about
a quarter inch wide giving me a peek at the interior.
What I could see up the center looked empty, but
full of light. At the far end a platform, with a portable blackboard, and in the gable behind it, high up,
a window or opening on the sky. I could see the
moon through it—or what looked like the moon. I
walked around to the back of the building to check
on what it was I was seeing but it was not the moon.
Whatever it was I had seen was on the window itself,
and not seen through it.

Behind a fence of wooden planks I had to rise on
my toes to see over, I saw a round, level plot of
ground, as sanded and smooth as a bullring, without an object or shadow of any kind to rest the eyes
on. It looked as if it had just been swept with a
broom. A playground? There was nothing to play
with. I felt kids might feel they were penned up in
it. A prison exercise yard would not have been so
vacant. I find it hard to describe what held my attention. A perfectly clean slate? A new and uncharted

beginning? Gazing at it I felt a surge of great expectations, but I've no idea for what. Crowds that wait in a piazza for someone to arrive must gather to share the same feeling. Their faces upturned, their eyes creased by the light. What holds them is the ceremony of waiting.

Perhaps that fence had been built to keep the children from the excavation behind it? What had they had in mind? The earth had been scooped out down to bedrock. Both the school and the playground could have been put into it, with room to spare. Perfectly round, from what I could judge, the earth had crumbled inward around the edges and there was a film of caked mud at the bottom. I turned away from it before I wondered what they had done with the dirt they excavated. Tons and tons of it. But there was no sign of it. It would be like Dahlberg, it seemed to me, or some other Swede, to get the idea there was treasure buried in this canyon. So they had dug and dug. When nothing turned up they decided to leave. As I walked back toward the car I thought there might well be a story in a town that wore itself out digging for treasure and just gave up.

I had my head down, to keep the sun out of my eyes, not glancing up until I noticed the shimmering shadow of a man on the hard baked street. It gave me a jolt. The figure stood between me and the light, a dark profile, holding the gun at a slant across his waist, the barrel pointed up.

"Howdy," he said. I couldn't speak. He looked taller than he was, thin in the shanks, with a hulking stoop to his shoulders. "You looking for someone?" A querulous, high-pitched voice. Nothing threatening. I was able to note that he wore tennis sneakers, without socks.

"Mr. Lorbeer," I said, "I thought I might catch him."

"You know Harry?"

"He's done some work for me."

"Well, he's not here. He's not often here daytimes. He keeps himself pretty busy daytimes."

"I was afraid of that," I said.

"What's your name?"

"Kelcey."

"I'll tell him you was by, Mr. Kelcey."

"Mr. Dahlberg's painting our deck," I said, aware that I was already saying too much. It was none of his business, whoever he was. The fright he had given me loosened my tongue. "You're a native?" I asked.

"I come up here"—he turned, showing his Adam's apple, wagging his finger down the river— "on the first trainload from Bixby. That's the Junction. We had a trainload to ourselves, just local people. I was nine years of age."

"There many of you?" I asked him.

He looked at me, cagily. "If I didn't patrol, we'd have the hoodlums in here. They'd haul it away like pack rats, the way they did Cheney. All they left of Cheney was the concrete around the filling stations." He had not answered my question.

"Well, I can believe that," I said.

"You better believe it," he said, and shifted his rifle from the left arm to the right arm. I thought he might be a relation of Dahlberg's. He might have straddled a rail fence without his thighs rubbing. In spite of his suspicious, vigilante manner I could see he welcomed a visitor, a chance to talk. "Yes sir-reee," he said, "you better believe it."

"Why would people leave a nice little town like this?" I peered up at a flight of big crows, their cawing echoed in the narrow canyon.

"They used to have wild turkeys in here. Anyhow, that's what they told us kids."

"I can guess why the turkeys took off—" I said.

"Back behind these trees we used to dig in the ash heaps left by Indians, fur trappers, horse rustlers. There used to be wild horses in this canyon. They set traps for wolves."

"And now there's just you, Mr. Lorbeer, and Mr. Dahlberg."

"More or less," he replied. I could see by the sidelong flick of his eyes that that question had been a mistake. He puckered his lips tight, as if he meant to spit.

"I want to tell you I envy you," I said. "I don't believe there's another place quite like it. You don't have the turkeys or the wild horses, but otherwise it's just like it used to be."

"Well, not *just.* We had seven hundred people, and as many as a thousand in here on some weekends. Those who moved away liked to come back. All summer long folks had family reunions. I guess I grew up thinking every place would be like it, the way you do."

"What happened?"

"Well, I suppose you would say it dated from the incident." I didn't want to push him. I let my gaze settle on the two railroad coaches backed up to the south end of the boardwalk. By accident or design the walk was at the same level as the floor of the coaches. You could step from one to the other. Topsoil and sand deposited by the river had settled in around the coach wheels, and concealed the tracks, so that it looked like a big double diner, closed down for the offseason.

"Someone could have made a diner out of that," I said.

"For who? Folks were leaving. Every train that come up had a flatcar attached to haul stuff away."

"It happened that fast?"

"You bet. One summer we had it crowded with people: the next summer it was almost like this. Not quite of course. Older people inclined to hang around until they died off."

"That's amazing," I said, "just because of one little incident."

"Oh, it wasn't so little. I didn't see it. I was in Fort Riley, taking basic training." He thought a moment. "I suppose I should let one of them tell it. Harry was here. He's the one to tell it."

"Too bad he isn't here," I said. "I see him so seldom."

"You go back to the war years and you'll find it reported. But with the war on it didn't arouse much interest. With so many people dead, so many missing, who cared about a handful here in Fork River?"

"How many is a handful?"

"They don't really know. There was so much confusion, when it was over, they don't know if they disappeared or just took off. Quite a few took off." What little he saw, he saw before him, wetting his lips. "The way they tell it is jumbled. Some say there was nothing but a roar like a jet, followed by a big whoosh. Others say it was one of these big funnels, bigger than any ever seen, that got its nose caught in the river canyon and just followed it along, sucking up all the water, to where it broke into the clearing right there behind the schoolhouse and sucked up the whole acre of the Victory garden, with the ten or twenty people who were working in it. Maybe more. You seen the hole?"

"It's like a crater."

"Well that's where everybody had their own piece of garden. They'd filled it all in with topsoil they found along the river, and used the river water to irrigate it."

"*That's* the story?"

"You can check it with Harry. He was here in town, but he wasn't near the garden. Some people ran around looking for people. Others just took off. The one certain thing, when it was all over, was that they had this hole in the ground and as many as ten or twenty people missing. Could be twice that number."

In the trees behind us a woodpecker hammered. It seemed so quiet in the street I could hear the heat rising. What I probably heard were bees thronging.

"You don't believe it?"

"That's a crater," I said, "not just a hole. All the dirt is removed down to bedrock. Tons and tons of dirt."

"Dahlberg's got the figures on it. It's a whale of a lot of dirt."

"It doesn't seem plausible," I said. "A twister just doesn't stop and drill a hole, like an auger."

"Most don't," he said, "but this one did. It came along to that point and just settled on it. People said they could hear it, like a big vacuum."

45

I tried to visualize it. "A big whoosh, right—?" I threw up my arms. "And then it all went through this hole in space?"

"Something like that. I didn't personally see it, but it's hard to believe the power in a big twister. You get one big enough it would suck you up a good-sized town, with all the people in it. I think what got people in a tizzy was that it might happen again, because of the river canyon. Like a vacuum nozzle stuck in a groove. The next time it might just suck up the whole town."

"It makes a good story."

"A body has yet to contradict it," he replied. I thought he was about to say, "and you can better believe it," but he held it back.

"I thank you for telling me. I might never have got it all out of Lorbeer. He seems to like his work."

"He keeps things shipshape around here. If somebody busts a window, he repairs it. There's nothing that you'd call run-down about it."

That there was not. Nor was there much run-down about him. I had the feeling he'd been waiting for me to arrive—I mean for years. As solid and suspicious as he seemed to be, I felt he might disappear if I took my eyes off him. "This Space Project," I said, "it's open on Sundays?"

"Yes sireeee, except in the winter. People find it hard to get in and out in the winter, but Harry likes to keep it open for interested people. They walk in

46

from the highway"—he gestured toward it—"or they hike in from Bixby, along the river. He seems to get a lot of the younger-type people. After the meeting they sit around in the grove, having a pic-nic." He said "in the grove" as if we were both standing in its shade. I understood that was just a way of speaking, since most of these trees were dead. The only leaves clung to the lower branches.

"What sort of meeting?" I asked. I found it hard to visualize.

"Oh, they just loll around, listening to the music, or they sit around looking at the pictures."

"He paints *pictures?*" I thought he might. I can't say that hearing that surprised me.

"Paints?" he replied. "I suppose he could. If it comes to his mind, he does it. They're big—" He spread his arms wide. "He gets them from the space and the weather people."

For a brief moment I thought I heard music: flocking birds spilled their shadows around us. "I've got to run along," I said, unmoving.

"I'll tell Harry you was here."

"I'll give him a call. We've got some work for him."

He watched me climb into and start the car. Thinking over what it was he had said to me, or I had said to him, he didn't wave. You may have no-ticed how people off the beaten path will stand and look at a stranger until he's out of sight, as if they doubted his existence. I went off slow. I thought he might fire over my head. To change my line of thought I wondered what Alice would say when I told her about the Space Project. Her eyes would dart about, as usual, then she would say, "It could be a tax shelter these days." That's the real world for you, as distinct from the one I had just left.

4

My FIRST WIFE often said of me, "Kelcey is a tease," without expanding on her meaning. If we happen to meet her somewhere she says to Alice, "Is he still a tease?" I should tell you we had known each other as children. Alice does not feel as I do about it since she considers the word a term of endearment. I have found that the phrase is favored by people who are guarded in their choice of words.

Alice is not guarded. She is small, but not petite. If she stands at my side my arm rests easily on her shoulders: with her right hand she often grips my thumb. Her eyes are brown, and so widely spaced they seem small. The dry summers out here chap her lips, which are usually slightly parted. Her hair is dark brown with bands of white at the temples her mother told me she was born with. She combines a rabbit-like, lettuce-nibbling shyness with inflexible assurance. In her absence, if I call her to mind, I usually see her crouched in the garden, wearing her green-thumb gloves, an indoor-outdoor house-plant. She likes to be rained on. The plight of the ladybugs is her study. On leaving the house to do her shopping I have heard her say, "Goodbye house!" There's a side to her nature it takes time to appreciate. All in all, I am not a bad judge of her feelings, but I would hesitate to say I know what she thinks. If the word "tease" can be applied to me, the word for Alice is *firm.*

In the early sixties I was a member of Seminars Afloat, summer cruises combining college-level courses. I had classes in history and journalism. Alice was one of the young teaching assistants who did most of the work. We sailed out of Barcelona at the end of June, and made stops at the less expensive places, Mallorca, Palermo, Corfu, Dubrovnik. Most of the time, of course, we were on the boat, and it was a long time. Alice seemed to be at ease with an older-type person, and I liked her independence and reserve. I remember wondering why such a pretty young thing so seldom smiled. Over the first winter she wrote me several letters, and the following summer she was back with the cruise. It seemed to me that I handled it all pretty well, considering. As a rule it is the young who arouse our expectations, but Alice, for one reason or another, associated hers with me. I was flattered. We were both concerned to avoid misunderstandings. She didn't write to me, over the second winter, but in June she was back in Barcelona, waiting for the boat. I detected in her manner a new assurance. For myself, I had been more or less alone for eight years, after a marriage that had lasted too long. The early sixties were still too early for "shacking up," a phrase that pretty well described such an arrangement, so we both had to face a difficult decision. With the summer over we stopped off in southern Indiana to see her mother. I had never heard Alice refer to her father. Mrs. Calley lived in the outskirts of New Albany, in a dense grove of trees overlooking the Ohio. On the plains you forget about the primeval forest, and cease to believe in it. It seemed to me as peaceful and pastoral as heaven. I felt like Hiawatha. Leaves luminous as fire lit up the floor of the woods, the sky veiled with blue streamers of fragrant leaf and wood smoke. I helped split a few logs. The sound went on ringing after I had stopped. Mrs. Calley was a tall, stooped woman, her steel gray hair drawn back so tight on her scalp it made her skin transparent. She wore a smock-like gray garment that hung to her ankles, lived in the oldest of the two frame buildings on the property. A wood-burning stove, but no lights. Shadeless oil lamps, with wicks curled in the oil, sat around the house smoking like votive candles. No rugs. No bureaus or bric-a-brac. Time moved sideways, ticking, or rose in circles. What she had in the way of possessions she left in the other house. My feeling is that neither house had ever been painted. The clapboards had the color of old barrel staves. One window in each of the three lower rooms. A door at the front and back. She sat in an armless, wicker-seated rocker, her arms folded at her front like braces, rocking without lifting her feet from the floor. She talked easily with her daughter, as if I wasn't there. Had the summer been hot? Were the foreign people friendly? In the Bible she had read that they all lived on fish.

The nights I lay awake on the cot upstairs had about them, for me, something unearthly. Bird cries. A deafening drone of insects. Pre-DDT in the planetary perspective. Something in my nature is unduly impressed with what has been sheared off, with the ultimately simple. It seemed to me the air I breathed was holy, like a loon's cry at Walden. Mrs. Calley kept a garden, she had friendly neighbors who often looked in on her, and chopped wood for her. Her busy work seemed to consist of the quilts and afghans she made over the winter to sell to the passing tourists over the summer. Some of them were spread out on a split rail fence that ran along the highway at her entrance. Fearing the worst about plains winters she insisted that Alice take one. It still smells of lamp oil.

Either Alice had several older brothers, or one older brother who had led several lives. Three or four of his abandoned and wrecked cars were back in the woods, half buried under leaves. He had driven a dog sled in Alaska, worked at mining in Australia, sailed out of New Orleans on freighters, explored caves in Kentucky, and tried his hand at mountain climbing, which he liked. Alice seemed reticent to talk about him. I sometimes wonder if he actually existed. As a youth he made a raft, right here on the farm, that he rode down the Ohio to the Mississippi, and down the Mississippi to New Orleans. As a big brother he impressed on her all the advantages of being a man. Her mother said to me, "Why, you're as tall as Leland," a seldom mentioned name. He seemed to be a tireless practical joker. Behind his ceaseless moving around was some intangible expectation. On that point brother and sister were much the same. Alice went to local schools, then to Chicago where she studied commercial art: she didn't know, at the time, there was any other kind. Her first job was to put in the hand-colored touches in a line of convalescent Get Well cards. Choosing the text for a line of cards in French and Spanish got her interested in languages. From there she made her way to the summer college cruises, and to me.

Does that seem a downward path of expectations? For three summers, I'm afraid, drifting at sea, with some legendary island on the horizon, I filled her ears with the fiction of the westward course of empire. It's quite a story, you know. The adventures of the Greeks were waterborne, as well as the Vikings and Columbus. They make tales suitable for growing boys. From the bluffs of the Missouri, looking west, the plains had once been an inland sea. Somehow they looked inviting. An illusion. All of that waving grass was nothing but a beachhead to the towering Rockies, and beyond the Rockies the infernos of sea-level valleys. Hell on earth. Why do so many dreams come out of such places? Is there one now hovering over Fork River? Think of it in 1840, unmapped and unknown, mountains alternating with burning deserts, month after month of danger and exhaustion, up ahead the maddening ripple of mirages, delirium cooling to cannibalism, the heat and sand to snow-clogged passes, amateurs, thieves, cranks, and visionaries making their lemming-like way to the goldfields. At once incredible and dismaying. The excursions of Alexander the Great, comparatively speaking, were like local raiding parties. The sea! the sea! was always there before them, off to one side, or behind them. To these demented landbound travelers the sea became an hallucination, a fevered state of mind. And yet in the time span of a childhood that vast territory had been *subjugated,* a word they loved. Translated that means: The dreamer has awakened. On the surface of the shrinking planet there would never again be a dream quite like it. Beneath it, perhaps, or above it. Next on the agenda loomed the sky. It had always been there, an inexhaustible fiction, a blackboard for speculation, mapped and remapped, made and unmade, but never explored. Conceivably, I said, in closing, man might set his foot on the moon.

"Not woman?" she asked. How well I remember that! A small correction in space tactics. We were huddled in the shelter of a lifeboat, to get out of the wind. Overhead the Mediterranean sky, strange to me, brought to mind none of my star maps. For all my talk I was an earthbound voyager. "Not woman?" she repeated.

"Why not?" I said, as if I might personally arrange it. My feeling was that she looked to me for something, but I'm not sure what. That fall, in Indiana, I had the impression that in this union I was contributing less than I would be receiving. Forest people have long spells of hibernation, interspersed with a passion for open spaces. I suppose you could say that Alice's early training—especially mine— seemed to look ahead, or sort of set her up, for Harry and Dahlberg. That's speculation, of course, as so much of my life increasingly seems to be.

We were watching the news when the phone rang, which usually means it's for Alice. She has a friend who calls her to make sure she doesn't miss anything.

"It's *her*," Alice said. She's not on the best of terms with Miss Ingalls.

"I hope I didn't disturb you," Miss Ingalls said. "I've uncovered something." She makes a nice distinction between uncover and discover. Uncover is touched with conspiracy. "You remember P. O. Bergdahl?" I did not. "I don't know how you writers solve anything," she said. "P. O. Bergdahl, the author of *Waiting*."

"Oh! *That* Bergdahl!"

"That Bergdahl," she repeated. "I've uncovered this picture—"

"Of Dahlberg?"

"—of this old soddy, Mr. Kelcey. It's out near Burwell. Mr. Bergdahl and his family are in front of it. I believe a man from Topeka took it. I don't know why they would let him. It's appalling. It's not the sort of picture you would show *any*-body. He has this child on his lap, with two women standing in the yard behind him."

"I'll be right over," I said. She took the time to assure me she would be there until nine o'clock. "She's turned up something," I said to Alice, "would you like me to drop you off at the Bergman movie?" It surprised me that she didn't.

56

"I'll just read," she replied.

I found Miss Ingalls at the checkout counter. She gave me a conspiratorial glance, then let me wait. On the desk in her office she had this file of early clippings and photographs. Miss Ingalls tells me that people now bring her pictures of the thirties, like old Bibles. They collect them like arrowheads or old flour sacks. They seem to have forgotten that Miss Ingalls had actually been there, a young woman in her twenties attending Teacher's College. The flour sack and the photograph are antiques. Neither Miss Ingalls nor I draw the obvious deduction.

The picture she handed me, the color of old newsprint, was mounted on gray board. It had the usual sepia tone of old photographs except for an object at the front, gleaming like false teeth. A big gross fellow sat there, wearing a collarless shirt, a doll-size child seated on his right ham. His weathered face and hands looked fire-blackened, his black tangled hair like a pelt. The impression I had had of gleaming false teeth was the keyboard of a portable house organ, the wind supplied by foot pedals. A blurred sheet of music was propped up on the rack. In the middle ground behind him, to his left and his right, two women dressed in black stood erect as columns. No visible features, brown hair drawn back to a tight knot at the nape of the neck, the hands crossed at the front as if covering an exposure. A trim of faded lace at the cuffs and throat. Behind them, set into a low mound, with a pile of manure heaped to the left, a sod house with a single black window, weeds or grain sprouting on the roof. The door stood ajar like the mouth of a cave. I can't explain what it was that riveted my attention. Was it the women, standing like icons, as if rejecting the connection between them, or the faceless, spread-legged hulk of the man exhibiting his valued possessions, a portable house organ, a frail, slightly blurred, tow-headed child.

"Good God!" I said.

"That's Ansell Bergdahl. One is Mrs. Bergdahl." She turned the picture over to check the names on the back. "The child on his knee is Peter O. Bergdahl. That would have been his father. I really don't blame him a bit. If I had people like that I'd change my name too."

The child appeared to take after the women, thin as a stick. In the blowing grass on the soddy roof I could see a pair of antlers and the horns of steers. I understood that this picture held a meaning that escaped me.

"He dreamed the whole thing up," I said. "I should have known it."

"Dreamed what up?"

I wagged my head in disbelief. "About his early life, the school he went to, the experience he had that changed his life."

58

"I should think he might. I'd dream something up too. You're a funny one to complain about people dreaming."

"I'm not complaining, Miss Ingalls. I'm just impressed by it. He did it so well he really took me in."

"They're a clever lot," she said. "His daddy was a self-taught wizard. He collected fossils. He knew all about sunspots. Mr. Rainey said he was one of the first to shoot off a rocket."

"Shoot off what?"

"Some sort of rocket. He was born before his time, according to Mr. Rainey."

At the bottom of the photograph someone had printed, in pencil,

A New Home on the Prairie
Settler takes Pride in his Possessions

Miss Ingalls took the photograph from my hands, but a ceremonial image remained on my mind's eye. Was it the organ or the child that was being sacrificed? "I simply don't understand how the women endured it," said Miss Ingalls. "Some of them didn't. They simply went crazy."

"And the men?"

"Oh, they could *do* things. They could shoot at each other. They could shoot off rockets." She gave me the smile of an accomplice, then added, "And some of them would grow up and write fiction."

Back at the desk I said, "Do you suppose you might have anything on a family named Lorbeer? A Harry Lorbeer?"

"I'll look into it, Mr. Kelcey," she said, "if I can just find the time."

5

HAVE YOU NOTICED that small, neatly turned young women are often attracted to gangly, uncouth, foot-in-the-mouth-type men? As well as the other way around? This morning he brought the morning paper up the drive with him, and just happened to meet Alice putting out the trash. My neighbor's wife would say they made a cute pair. He took a moment to point out a small local item to her, although nothing interests Alice less than the local news. She has always had a peculiar distaste for reports of the sort that she has just brought into the house, clipped out, and read to me.

500 BIRDS
DROP DEAD

Liggett

Blair County

Birds were dropping dead from the telephone wires in Blair County. Tim Conroy stopped his car to pick a few of them up. He said they looked normal enough, except they were dead. Conroy is one of Blair County's bird watchers. He identified the birds, of the blackbird family, as being strange to the area. They had blown off their course, lost their way, gone crazy, or something. He took several of the bird bodies to the State Fish and Game people in Liggett for analysis.

Two weeks ago she would have said, "That's your stinking, awful bomb!" Now she said nothing.

I said, "Must have been something they ate."

"You want to know what he said? He said if he was a bird, out in that dismal country, he would have dropped dead long ago. There's not a tree in it. What is a poor bird to do? Nothing but these awful wires for them to roost on. Imagine seeing it all as clearly as they do!"

"They're *birds*," I said, "they're free to take off. We've got trees right here if they're looking for trees. Who told them to go out there and sit on the wires?"

"That's what he wants to know. He's sure they know something we don't."

She left me to think that over. A moment later she was back to retrieve the clipping.

"Alice," I said, "it's not all that unusual. They could have eaten some poisoned grain or something."

"Is that so usual?" she replied, and I've been sitting here reflecting on it. I know the country around Liggett. If you could put what is left out there on a truck and take it anywhere else it would be an antique. Before motels came in they used to have tourist cabins about the size of tool sheds. You parked your car in the space between them. On the windy days dust puffed up, like smoke, through the cracks in the floor. Around Liggett, when the dust was blowing, you might see cars with windshields like pieces of frosted glass, the paint sandblasted off the windward side. One thing I would like to tell Alice is that not only birds drop dead out there. I remember an old woman, out in the yard, her skirts blowing and flapping like wash on a line. A common turn of speech, if you can get one of them to talk, is the phrase "in all of my born days," followed by "I never saw anything like it." Birds dropping off wires would not receive much comment. Birds that *stayed* on the wires would be cause for wonder. What I would like to tell Alice is that the craziest happenings are best described in the plainest language. If you see birds dropping dead, you say so. If you see someone walking on water, you just say so. If you see a hole in the sky, you say so. But if you see a flying object, unidentified, floating in over the treetops like a Frisbee, my advice would be to keep it to yourself.

Dahlberg stopped painting at four o'clock to work on a trellis for Alice's tomatoes. He thinks better of me now that he knows my saw is sharp. What is he thinking? I see only the back of his knobby head. I would have said his mind was a restful blank, like a farmer at the end of a plowed furrow, but knowing him as the author of *A Hole in Space* I see his brain pan twinkling like a constellation. Where is he off to? He envys me Alice. I envy the private world of his hands. One dangles like the claw of a machine, the thumb delicately tapping the second finger (a hangover of the days he dusted his cigarette); the other he has placed at the small of his back with the palm turned outward, the fingers paint-smeared. I can see that hand is anxious to get back to work. Whatever *he* is thinking it is eager to grip, heft, or touch something. If it knew what was on his mind it would make a swipe at the back of his head, as if rubbing a crystal ball. Dahlberg drinks from the hose, holding it upright, taking little slurps from the side. He is at once ungainly and fastidious. When his face is wet his eyelashes tangle and he looks very boyish.

I offered Dahlberg a beer, while he waited for Harry, and we sat on the part of the deck that had dried. I angled for an opening to bring up Fork River, but with me he gets defensive. Wouldn't it be

64

more convenient, I asked him, if they lived closer to the city? He didn't think so. If I hinted I had found and read one of his books, I would never see him again. If the chance offered, I thought it might be possible to discuss Fork River with Harry Lorbeer, who would not take it so personally. After all, he had put his name on a project that seemed to relate to the town's curious history. I considered it characteristic that Dahlberg's name had not been on it.

Harry Lorbeer was late, coming all the way from Crete, and honked at the end of the driveway for Dahlberg. "If you can find the time," I asked him, "we'd also like you to paint the garage door." The deck and the garage are both a gunmetal color, and use the same paint. I hope he appreciated that I did not ask if he'd be back in the morning.

"How did you two get along today?" I asked Alice. She'd picked up a little sunburn working in the garden. I knew they had got along very well, but she was weighing the intent of my question. It's a great challenge to feel that familiar motives have become complex. She had never had to guess at what I was thinking. Now she did.

"He's traveled. He's been to Italy." I said nothing. "And he was in the war."

"What war? That's hard to believe."

"Why is it hard?"

"I mean about the war. I don't see Dahlberg in a war."

"I don't see you in one either, and you were. He liked Italy but not the Italians."

"What did you say to that?" Alice makes a point of liking Italians, to justify her dislike of the Germans and the French. The Italians are more "human." They go through your bags while you're asleep.

"He thinks life is a joke," Alice said.

"He thinks *what?*" We were out on the deck. It seemed particularly foolish to hear that on the deck. We could see across the plain almost to Kansas.

"No, I think he said *hoax.* Life on this planet is a hoax."

"Oh my God," I said. "The thinking man's house painter."

"The thinking *woman*'s house painter," she corrected.

"He said, life on this planet?"

"I did think that was silly."

"I take it he's had encouraging word from one of the others, right?"

"He wasn't just griping. He's really thought about it. I know it isn't so stupid as I've made it sound."

"I'll schedule a conference," I said, "I'm not too clear about these innovations. Imagine getting all this for three bucks an hour."

My sarcasm reassured her, showing her how much I cared.

66

"So how was *your* day?"

"No new planets," I said, "but talk of an old twister. They say this one followed along the Fork River to where it sucked up twenty or thirty people. They just disappeared."

"They scare me to death," she replied, and I knew that. The one thing she had insisted about the house was a basement.

"Not only people," I continued, "but real estate, including a new Victory garden. It left a hole like a mini-crater." I had the clear impression she had stopped listening. People who live in California shudder to hear about twisters: people familiar with twisters tremble to hear about quakes. Alice couldn't bear to hear about either of them. "I took a run out to look at it," I went on. "They call it Fork River. Except for the hole there's no sign that anything hit it. It's like a ghost town. The people just packed up and took off."

"I should think they would," said Alice.

"A self-respecting twister doesn't just drill a hole like that, then stop. It looks like it might have been made by an auger. It's not plausible."

"The poor people must have found it plausible. Why don't you ask Mr. Dahlberg?"

"I thought *you* might ask him. That you'd heard about this twister in Fork River. See what he says. If I ask him he'll clam up."

"Why shouldn't he tell you, if it's such a special twister?"

"There's just the two of them," I said, "in this ghost town. Flocks of cawing crows, a sort of lost world feeling. My feeling is they would like to keep it special."

"You're not thinking of doing a piece on it?"

"When something drops right in my lap," I replied, "I can't help but think about it. I don't know what I'm thinking. It's a subject that has some interesting angles. People are more open to unusual happenings than they used to be."

She knew I was covering something, but she wanted me to feel that she didn't know it.

"Is a twister so unusual?"

"The people in Fork River seemed to think so. After this incident, which is what they call it, they packed up and cleared out as if the place was cursed. They did not come back."

"If he brings it up, we'll discuss it. I am not going to pry into his background."

"Fine," I said. Knowing Alice I knew that she would, if I could keep Dahlberg around long enough. If he was talking about his travels already, he would get to Fork River sooner or later.

"While we've got him around," I said, "I've asked him to do the garage door. He's a good painter. You have anything you'd like Harry to look at?"

"Harry who?"

68

"Mr. Lorbeer. People refer to him as Harry."

"I'd like another bathroom," she said, "but I don't know where to put it."

"Contractors have these portable outbillies," I said. "We could rent one and put it at the foot of the garden."

Alice left me with the paper, and as I checked the weather it occurred to me that the Fork River twister—if that was what it was—should have been reported in the local journal. If Dahlberg came to work, interrupting my concentration, I might check back on the Heber County weather, during the war.

Dahlberg did not appear for work. I found that more of a distraction than if he had, since it magnified his rudeness. He knew to what extent this affected my work. Allowing for the fact that that might amuse him, he was equally rude to Alice. How little trouble it would have been for him to call and explain. At twenty minutes to eleven I phoned Fork River with a few good lines for their answering service. Dahlberg answered. On the phone he had a high pipsqueak voice. "Is it any of our business," I said, "why you have decided not to appear?"

"No," he replied. That found me at a disadvantage. I was certain he would give one excuse or another.

"Alice is anxious about her tomatoes. She's been waiting weeks for that trellis."

"I'll try to make it tomorrow."

"Is Harry there?" I asked.

"He's busy."

Having been there, having looked the place over and found it as dead as a cemetery, I appreciated his comment. "If he can find the time, I'd like him to call me. There's something I'd like to ask him."

"I'll tell him." Just by the voice and manner I would have thought I was talking to a child, about six years old. I hung up before he could hang up on me.

"For unmitigated rudeness and insolence . . . You heard me tell him you were waiting for your trellis."

"I am not *waiting*, and he knows that. The vines aren't long enough for a trellis."

"All he had to do was give you a call. I've already told him to reverse the charges."

About noon, having had no call, I drove in to the college campus. We have this great institution of learning which trains and exhibits a football team. You will have heard of the team. If a big cornfed local boy has heard of the team, just try and keep him down on the farm. In the fall one of my neighbors, a successful dentist, hangs a banner across the front of his house, screening off the picture window, which reads GO BIG RED. He loves it. His kids love it. He tells me that his wife loves it. On home-game weekends they wear red hats, ties, and jackets, and walk around like Irish children at their first communion. When we speak of an agricultural state, we mean one that grows big cornfed beef, on the foot and on the hoof. The local weather forecasts are as important as the oracles at Delphi. I had met the chief weatherman, socially, and found him agreeably full of his subject: a man who loves his work. Fred Rainey was also about my own age, and would remember—if there had been one—the incident at Fork River. He knew of me as the author of a piece looking hopefully forward to the next ice age. He loves ice ages. If there's a drop in the global temperature I hear from him.

"Sure," he said to his secretary, "send him in."

Another secretary, an elderly woman, sits at the back of his office wearing earphones, taking dictation from a tape deck. She didn't seem to be aware that I had entered the room. Dr. Rainey is a big, hulking man who belongs outdoors, but finds himself trapped indoors. He gets out just enough to keep a light tan on his face and hands. I felt almost indecently casual when I saw him, since I was wearing summer slacks, with a short-sleeved shirt, and open-weave, flat-soled sandals; he was buttoned into a dark brown suit that was too small for him. Including the vest. It's not often you see the coat and the vest. Rainey has just never had the excuse to depart from the customs he was raised in, such as cupping the elbow of your wife when you lead her down the walk to your car, or up the aisle of a movie house. As I came in I saw him tap out a lozenge from the packet in the drawer of his desk, pop it into his mouth.

"How are you, Kelcey?" he boomed, and pushed his chair back from the desk, so he could tilt back in it. His office is now air-conditioned, and I could feel a cool draft blowing on me from somewhere. Soon I would sneeze. I said I was fine, and what I wanted to ask him, if he had the time, was a little bit about twisters. Everybody in this state is interested in the weather, and if they stay long enough they get an interest in twisters. There is nothing in nature equal to them. The hurricane is more powerful, especially at sea, but you know well in advance if one is coming, and what to expect. The earthquake is as sudden, and more unnerving, but it's the aftereffects you remember. I've been in quakes, and watched the chandeliers swing in a theater full of people. A quake is not much without the panic, and the crumbling walls. With a little luck out here in twister country, you can see the funnel shape up on the horizon, dipping and swaying, or a pillar-like column that is almost transparent, like a rain falling, but not frayed off like rain at the edges, and long before you hear it like a downgrade freight train you feel it in what my father called the *withers*. The terror you feel is primeval. It centers in the guts and radiates along the nerve wires. The hairs prickle at their roots. The fingers tingle. In the split of a second you're an animal in panic, either paralyzed or running for its life. In my boyhood most of the houses that didn't have basements had a storm cave, a mound of dirt in the yard with a cave beneath it. It didn't freeze in the winter and it was cool in the summer. People used it to store potatoes, fruits and jellies, churned butter. I remember my mother, crouched on a sack of onions, hugging me to her breasts so I could feel her heart throb. Nothing happened. I was carried back upstairs and was soon asleep.

"Anything in particular?" he asked me. His hands were clasped behind his head, rumpling his hair. Rainey married a local girl, who blessed him with four daughters, then returned to her position as a high school science teacher. Alice and I sometimes see them at the shopping plaza, or driving home from church. He will say, "Give my regards to Mrs. Kelcey," when I leave. I'll thank him and say, "Give our best to Mrs. Rainey." I have heard him say that when people cease to do that, the game is up.

"You happen to recall the Fork River twister?"

He had been tilted back, savoring his lozenge. He tilted forward and looked at me over the rim of his glasses. "Where did you run into that?"

"It just so happens," I said, "we've got a fellow painting the deck from Fork River. I'd never heard of it and couldn't find it on the highway road maps, but Miss Ingalls, at the library, found it for me just below the Kansas state line." I could see that he was waiting for me to go on. "The story seems to be that it was a thriving town, mostly Swedes, until the incident of the twister. It frightened people so bad they packed up and took off."

Rainey tilted forward to open his desk drawer, find a paper clip, unbend it so he could use it to clean his nails. I thought of Harry, and his wire coat hangers.

"That's all hearsay," I said. "Is that how you recall it?"

He removed his glasses and polished the lenses with his tie. "During the war," he said, "I was in Washington. I didn't get back here till it was over." That's what you call a cardiac bypass.

"It's all history now," I said, "the place is like a ghost town. This house painter and his friend have it all to themselves. It must have been one of the nicest places in the state until the twister struck and the people panicked. The story is that quite a number of the natives were at work in the community Victory garden, just behind the school. The school looks fine. Just behind it, up the canyon, is this hole like a small crater. Almost perfectly round. The sides so smooth that if you fell in it you might have a time getting out. No dirt anywhere. What sort of twister drills a hole like that?"

I tried to look suitably wonderstruck about it, anxious to know the exact name of this marvel. He wheeled his chair around so that he faced the louvres at the window. He's up about four floors, and has a good view of the plain, if he wants it.

"Twisters don't drill holes," he said, "—as a rule."

"That was my own impression. You'd have to get the twister to stop right there, like the nozzle was stuck, and suck up the soil like a soft drink through a straw."

"That's a nice metaphor, Kelcey."

"I don't want to use it if it's not accurate."

"It's a vacuum," said Rainey, "on the human scale. The twister is a vacuum on the planetary scale. If you got one just a little bit bigger I suppose you could suck up anything that wasn't nailed down."

"Would you say that was highly unlikely?"

In the pause I could hear the clack-clack of his secretary's typewriter. The earphones gave her the aspect of a preoccupied spaceship pilot. Where was she off to? The reels wheeled on the tape deck.

"Would you say it was highly unlikely, Kelcey, to have a dinosaur put his head through the window?"

"I guess I would." I nodded.

"You get your time systems out of phase, and it would be more or less normal. You get your physical systems out of phase and you might get one hell of a vacuum, right out of the blue."

"Right out of the blue?"

"Why not? It's a smear of air around this planet, Kelcey, no thicker than the skin of your teeth. You prick it with something and you've got a vacuum."

"Rainey," I said, "what have you been reading?"

"It relaxes me," he replied, "more than the weather."

"Did you ever happen to read one titled *A Hole in Space?*"

Rainey's solemn, fleshy face is often like that of a Buddha. Meditative, without a clue to what he was thinking. "Is it a good one? I like the title."

"My current house and deck painter wrote it. His name is O. P. Dahlberg."

When you are testing melons for ripeness you want the one that rings hollow. I had hit it. Rainey picked at the lint on the sleeve of his coat. "You happen to know a P. O. Bergdahl?" I asked him.

Rainey said, "What were you reading?"

"Miss Ingalls mentioned him to me."

"A sort of wunderkind, Kelcey. Grassroots whizz-kid. One of the first to relate sunspots and tree rings. Collected meteorites. Wrote a paper suggesting they might be flying objects. Designed and shot off a rocket."

"What became of him?"

"Working on a new rocket propellant he made a miscalculation."

We were silent. His secretary, clamped between

her headphones, ticked away in her familiar orbit. At some point in every discussion you know you have come full circle. Just a few remarks back we were both headed outward: here we were back with the flying objects. At the door I turned and said, "Doesn't that damned typing get on your nerves?"

"Cuts down on the idle speculation," he replied.

"I just thought of something," I said. "What became of the rocket?"

Rainey peeled back the foil on a pack of fruit drops, pried one loose. "There's two points of view, Kelcey. You can settle for a theory that tells you what can't happen—or you can see what happens and forget the theory."

"That reminds me of the Fork River Space Project," I said.

"Fork River *what?*"

"Space Project. They meet on Sundays. I understand they listen to music and go into orbit." Rainey had tilted back to look at the reflections cast by the venetian blinds on the ceiling. "I sometimes get the feeling the old ball game is over. You ever feel like that?"

He wheeled his chair to face the glare at the windows. The prevailing wind had tilted the trees so that a gale appeared to be blowing.

"How do we start a new game, chum?" he asked

me. Chum is the word he uses in a friendly put-
down.

"The man to see is Dahlberg," I said, "if you
catch him in time."

6

THERE'S NOT MUCH TO BE DONE with a hole but look at it. The cooling of the globe, the creation of the seas, the coming and going of the ice, the dinosaurs, and the Progressive Party were all reasonable acts compared to the mini-crater on the Fork River.

What did Harry Lorbeer mean by a *space project?* Instead of acting on the sly, to appease Dahlberg, which so far had got me nowhere, I should persuade Alice to go along with me and drive out to Fork River on Sunday. The Project was open from 2 to 5. There were questions I would like to put to Harry, knowing I would get nothing out of Dahlberg. If we appeared on Sunday with the others, there would be nothing underhand about it. I would

79

let Alice break the news to Dahlberg if she would rather that we didn't surprise him. I'd actually like to hike up the river myself, but it wouldn't suit Alice. "You hike, darling, then tell me what it was like."

On Friday we had Dahlberg from 10:00 to 2:30, at which time he had completed the deck. I walked out to admire what he had done, which was not hard, since he is a good painter. He made no objection to being admired, but neither did he appreciate the effort it cost me. He's a clever fellow. He knew very well that Alice had put me up to it. He had only bought paint enough for the deck, so he would have to wait till Monday to start on the trim. He has mannerisms, when I am talking to him, that make it hard for me to be civil. One thing he does is screw his little finger into his ear right up to the second knuckle, grimacing as if it pained him. It could be a trick. He does it in a way that implies he finds it hard to hear me. I've already mentioned how he stands, looking away. Until I caught on to that one I would move to see what it was he was observing. He implied this was none of my business. The truth is that Dahlberg finds it hard to conceal his infatuation for Alice, his jealousy of me. This gives me a certain edge, a leverage, so to speak, I didn't have at the start. It led me to say, "I've been reading about Fork River. It's got quite a history. I'm thinking of driving Alice over to see it. Would Sunday be a good day?"

"How would I know that?" he replied. Sensing I had the advantage I felt different about his rudeness. "Well, if it happens to be, maybe we'll drive over. How long does it take?"

"You ought to know," he said, "since you've driven it."

I was willing to be caught in that lie to determine if the old man had reported my visit.

"I found the road pretty bad," I said, calmly. "Is there a better way to get in and out?"

"Some walk," he replied. "They walk up from Bixby, about seven miles."

"That's fourteen miles. I don't think Alice would like it."

He gave me a sidelong glance, from the feet upward, implying that a person with longer legs would set a good example for Alice to follow. Dahlberg has the mannerisms, when he feels imposed on, of an aging rock singer bored with bobby-soxers. I'm puzzled why Alice finds this sort of thing appealing, since her taste has always been for mature-type men. My feeling is that what she enjoys is playing Dahlberg off against me. After all, he is only her second man.

While waiting for Harry to arrive with the van we sat on the deck, listening to Italian conversation records. Alice speaks excellent French, but her Italian, as she said to Dahlberg, was "rusty." She "knew" Italian (having got an A in the course) but she feared to speak it and make a fool of herself. I did not know it, and rattled it off pretty well. It had taken the bloom off our month in Portofino. She had so wanted to be my interpreter and guide, but she clammed up.

If the two of them knew Italian as well as they knew English neither of them would have said much more than *prego*, but a smattering of some language seems to encourage duffers to speak it. Alice had more assurance than she had had in the past, and Dahlberg was an eager, appreciative pupil. He had never before sat on a deck listening to a young woman speak at him in Italian. Did he plan to go to Italy? No, not at the moment. It had been Alice's idea. They had got to talking about Perugia, where they had both been, and Venice, where they hadn't, and places like Sardinia they were eager to go to, and all that crazy country in the heel of the boot that the tourists had not yet got to.

Had either of them read *Old Calabria?* I asked. They had not. Until that moment I had not re-marked anything complicit in their glances. At that moment I did. It was a veiled glance that plainly said, "Oh, *him!*" I was more amused by that than irritated because as you grow older it gets to be so common. To have read a few good books dates you. Have you noticed that?

The FM playing in the room behind us suddenly switched from guitar to orchestral music. A glowing surge of sound, like dawn breaking. Berlioz, Wagner, or one of the Russians. I stepped inside for a moment to turn up the volume, then came back to the deck to listen. Perhaps I *am* a little obsessed on the subject. A thin, tremulous, reed-like tone seemed to penetrate my ears and stay there, as if trapped in my head.

"You hear that?" I said. "That's Borodin. Russian space music. 'On the Steppes of Central Asia,' wherever that is. As I understand it, the steppes are open country." I gestured to the south, the wide view we have of it. It was one of those days we can see into Kansas, or rather over it. It was Kansas that spread out below me, with the visible tracings of the pack ice. "Hear that?" I said.

Alice said, "Hear what?"

"That tone, that reed-like sound." I put my index fingers to the tips of my thumbs and drew a long thin line on the air before me. With half-lidded eyes I attempted to whistle. Nothing occurred.

Dahlberg said, "Do we see, or hear it?"

"Listen!" I said, but what I heard may have been in my ears. It thinned to a sliver that gleamed like a knife blade. Alice eyed me with some apprehension. "It's not *just* a sound—" I said.

"Then what is it?"

"Well—" I said, "for one thing, it's like a space signal."

Was I right in feeling they exchanged glances?

83

"You're expecting one?" asked Alice.

I went back inside to turn up the volume, but the reed-like tone had vanished. It's what you hear in the ascending lisp of a saw, just as it dies off. Thinking it might come again I waited. I once had, but lost, the power to move my ears. Signals were whooshing past me all the time that a sleeping cat would capture and analyze later. Through the window I watched Dahlberg pour himself some Campari, a sweet vermouth they advertise on café umbrellas. It was not lost on me that he was more assured.

A loud honking in the street proved to be Harry Lorbeer, who had come by to pick up Dahlberg. Alice wanted him to come to the deck and join us, but fortunately he was too tired. From the deck we watched Dahlberg walk down the drive, his elbows up from his side, as if his arms were wet, a space between his legs you could ride a bike through. Just as he climbed into the car I yelled, "See you on Sunday!" but I'm not sure he heard me. He could always hear you, if he thought it to his interest, or he could wonder to what you had reference. His expression is the one you see on the dog on the gramophone horn.

I stayed in the drive for a while, sweeping leaves, watching the Mafia-type jays dominate the bird feeder, giving Alice time to clear away the glasses and make her way back from Perugia. When I entered the house she gave me a detached Mona Lisa smile.

7

UNABLE TO CONCEAL her satisfaction Alice brought another clipping back to my study. She placed it on my desk without comment.

BIRDS KEEP DYING

Liggett

Blair County

More birds fell from their roosts in and near Liggett over the past few days. Some observers report finding birds in the open fields, where there was nothing to fall from but the sky.

"I think they probably picked up some kind of poison," said Wayne Dorrance, of the Fish and Game Dept. He said an infestation of one thing often led to another. He did not elaborate.

Why is this bad news for birds good news for Alice? She sees it as a triumph of the unlikely. Things were going well if they remained mysterious. Was she beginning to see, like me, what was on the lids of her eyes? Would it surprise me to hear from her in space? In all soberness I ask the question in the hope it will help me face it.

In the mail this morning I received an article from Miss Ingalls. "Time Warp," by P. O. Bergdahl. She found it in a magazine devoted to local history and train buffs. It was published in the spring of 1958, on high-quality, glossy-stock paper, selected to enhance the illustrations, provided by H. L. Lorbeer.

The writer tells how trappers and buffalo hunters used to spend their winters at the fork of the river before it had a name. In the ashes of their campsites, a century later, he had found the bones they had gnawed on. Lead bullets and arrowheads were easier to find than the location of the fork of the river. The first order of business was to get it on a map. To get it on the map was to make a beginning.

Everything in the state, once it became a state, or in the unmapped regions west of the Missouri, had a beginning as clearly defined as the heavens and the earth in scripture. One day it wasn't there at all: the next day it was "discovered." The writer asks in passing, "Was the discovery of America a mistake?" The systematic looting, polluting, exploiting, followed on the "discovery" as night follows day. That marked the beginning. The trapper and his traps, the wagon trains headed for the goldfields. Was it a beginning to be celebrated or an ending to be mourned? At that point in his article, as well as in time, the writer asked that question in hope of an answer. He wanted to know.

All animals leave traces (he goes on) but few can compare with the leavings of man. In a gravesite on the rim of the canyon, a fully clad body was found with the toes sticking out of his boots. He lay on his face, the toes of his shoes were worn away by the hole he had been digging to crawl into. Once you left the canyon for the open plain there was no place to hide.

Some time after the turn of the century a Colonel Lorbeer, on a surveying trip out of Bixby, Kansas, came up the river to spend an unforgettable night at the fork. That was how he described it to Olivia Bayliss, his prospective bride. The Colonel had camped in a grove of trees, under a canopy of stars. Through the night he heard the water purling. His bride-to-be had often mentioned her love of water and trees. An Eastern girl, she was spending that summer at the Dells in Wisconsin. She had never been west of Rockford, Illinois. She thought wherever he was sounded delightful, and asked him if it offered a view of the mountains. That letter, and that question, went unanswered. In others she wrote to the Colonel he gathered that the thought of the "open" treeless plains distressed her. What *was* there where it was open? Was there nothing but buffaloes and Indians? He reassured her that with the coming of the railroad, with the coming of progress, with the coming of a woman like herself all of that was history. He was a maker of history, being nothing if not a man of his time.

Fork River proved to be a town created for the bride of a railroad mogul. The man who builds, as the Colonel did, a nine-mile spur of railroad up a dead-end canyon for the convenience of his wife has what we call panache, and is not without interest. She liked trees and the sound of running water, and that was what she got. The article is illustrated with a map, some drawings, old photographs, and a snapshot of the author. It's him, all right. He sits on the boardwalk in front of the stores with his bare feet dangling in the flooding water, a Fork River Huck Finn.

The writer gives the impression that he knew Olivia Bayliss, the Colonel's wife. There's a picture of her, a flattering soft-focus portrait in the turn-of-the-century manner. Soulful eyes, billowy light brown hair gathered in a loose and improvised manner. The well-brought-up children—three girls and one boy—often stood at the door while she fussed with her hair. The bone hairpins between her teeth made it hard to follow her instructions. A very up-to-date man, and an empire builder, the Colonel wanted, but did not get, an old-fashioned girl. She was several inches taller, musically gifted, a flighty creature who needed to be hooded, like a falcon. (The writer actually says that.) She wore (he tells us) long strands of beads that she worked like pulleys when the conversation was animated. If it was dull she might protrude her lip and twist strands of her hair to droop like a moustache. These are all things, of course, a child would remember. She kept a butterfly collection in glass cases, played Mah Jong with her children, shot off the Colonel's pistols. But the long summers were a heat-tossed sleep. The Colonel let her spend some of them in England, from where she wrote him letters he found it hard to decipher. Did he cycle? she asked him. Wouldn't a little exercise do him good? The letter clearly suggested she expected it of him. The word *expected* was so appropriate to Olivia that the Colonel felt obliged to fulfill her expectations. They cycled in France. There is a snapshot of the Colonel wearing plus fours and a cyclist's cap. Shortly after they return to Fork River, however, Olivia is afflicted with a "nervous ailment." It took the form of laryngitis. She could not speak in a manner they could understand. The children and her husband were obliged to read her lips. Years later it led her son, Harry, to interesting speculations about sign language on the plains. What led it to arise? The problems of space. The human voice simply didn't carry. At the distance it was safe for strangers to meet shouting was pointless: so signs developed. The antelope, indigenous to the plains, exposed the white underparts of his tail to signal a warning. The writer does not elaborate on what it was Olivia Lorbeer was trying to signal. Harry remembers her often saying to her husband, "Please don't shout!" The girls were sent to school in the East, when they were old enough to travel, but Harry stayed at home with his mother. Did she need him? Was he a loner? He remembers sitting with her at the table under a cone of light that concealed all of his father but his hands. The effect on the boy was like that of a seance, mysterious, disembodied movements. A servant, named Jackson, a former dining car porter, cooked the food and served it wearing a white porter's jacket. The boy saw the jacket moving about the table, but not the hands.

It all makes good reading, with the illustrations. It shows to advantage the writer's early talent in blending fact and fiction. I recognize both, having been partially there myself. Just a few hours away, in Omaha, I was caught up in the adventures of Douglas Fairbanks and Tom Mix. Those were palmy days! My father was into real estate, the Orpheum Circuit, and chick incubators in Shenandoah, Iowa. What about Harry Lorbeer? Had he come too late for crystal sets and winding his own coils around Quaker Oats boxes? The last of the

Colonel's four children, he was schooled by the depression. The Wild West was receding, like a view down the tracks, and he had his first taste of lip reading. From both sides of his background he inherited a talent for fiction. How would he apply it? The one thing he saw the most of was the sky. But these are my speculations, not the author's, and his subject is the rise and fall of Fork River.

The men who turned the century built railroads the way we now build freeways. A well-traveled man, the Colonel wanted a house that combined the best of the East and the West. The wide, run-around porches, with the gazebo-like bulges of the country homes that would soon become resorts, with the sprawling comfort of western haciendas. He kept it low to stay in the shelter of the canyon. Bay windows as wide as those of a Pullman diner, red tiles on the roof. I know how he felt. I once dated a girl who lived in such a home in Waukegan. The deep porch surrounded it with a moat of darkness. In the evening I could see her at the piano, her mother seated under a lamp with a beaded shade, sewing. In the dark of the porch a creaking hammock. What a time her evil-minded little brothers gave me. No matter where we were I could hear them giggling like fiends. I loved the house. It was the house I missed when we broke up. Just using the elegant, spacious bathrooms, with towels as large and fleecy as rugs, gave me my first taste of perishable grandeur. Was it the same with Harry? In a summer storm, in the thirties, the Colonel's house was struck by lightning and burned to the ground. That explains the empty space behind the meeting house, fenced off from everything else like a helicopter landing.

There is a picture of the Colonel, the empire builder, standing on the rear platform of the first train to enter Fork River. Lesser dignitaries are ranked behind him. The rear platform of a club car was the best pulpit for a substantial public figure. The Colonel was substantial. His open stance, fingers hooked in his vest, was loosely defined as "presence." He had it. William Jennings Bryan had it. An uncle on my mother's side had it, but missed the train. Very little of Fork River is visible behind him, but enough to appreciate the changes. The present meeting house, or church, was not there. In the space that is open behind it sat the house he had built for his wife. Among the cottonwoods and poplars along the south bank it is possible to see the first "company" houses, as they were called. Either the railroad or the Colonel provided the money to encourage people to settle at the Fork. All the houses were white frame buildings with two or three bedrooms, lightning rods, and no basements. Thanks to the railroad they didn't need cars. The block of business structures, set up on stilts, was dictated by the seasonal rise of the river. Shortly after the fire the Colonel moved his family to Colorado Springs. It was a fashionable spa at the time, and Mrs. Lorbeer had had enough of Fork River. The children adored it but she found the winters long.

Until the market crash the town flourished, but that put the skids to the railroad empire. I can imagine they began to close down on the mortgages. As the depression deepened everything cut back, and most of the people in Fork River were laid off. Some hung on, of course, assuming that they would soon go back to work. Even the weather changed. There were crop failures and dust bowls. I remember days, traveling from east to west, that it was as dark at high noon as at dusk. Many of the younger people, understandably, took off. During the Second World War Fork River was bypassed. The train no longer ran in and out. Mr. Lindner continued to live there, and for part of the time, at least, Harry Lorbeer. I learned from Jake, at the gas station in Millard, that after the twister Harry used to drive in and out in a jeep. I've no idea as yet when Dahlberg joined him, but I would guess the late fifties. I'd like to have seen that occasion. Two oddballs that manage to roll into the same pocket. It does happen. Oddball people should know that and take heart.

I don't find it hard to see Harry, a typical sort of loner, learning to make do in Fork River. It's the boy who sits alone, in the hollow of a rock, or staring at the ashes in a dying fire, who sees unheard of things when he lifts his eyes and looks around him. Where does he look? In the Fork River canyon he looked at the sky. I recall dimly, for just a flickering moment, my own bafflement that it was so empty all day, and so crowded at night. That's a wondrous thought. A mind like P. O. Bergdahl's, or O. P. Dahlberg's, might have made something out of it. I suspect it was Dahlberg who gave Harry the clue to changing the world. You just renovate it, reassemble the parts to heart's desire. What I'm afraid of is that Dahlberg's faculty for fiction is going to make my own problem harder. He imagines what he pleases. He has no respect at all for the facts. How am I, or how is Alice for that matter, ever to know when he is speaking the truth? It seems reasonably certain Bergdahl was his father, but how be sure? Among his father's many remarkable talents was a gift for fabrication. I use the word advisedly. Fictions were his stock-in-trade. This somewhat circumstantial tie is the strongest link between father and son. Congenital liars? It's hard to draw a clear line on the blue of the sky, or the green of the sea. They lived together, briefly, in Omaha, where P. O. Bergdahl is identified as a graduate of the Technical High School. Ten years later he surfaces as O. P. Dahlberg, author of *The Taste of Blood*. There isn't the faintest evidence he ever lived in Provo, Utah, had Mormon parents, or went to school in Walla

Walla. There may be a fact in his reading *The Grapes of Wrath* and getting a hangup over the turtle. The rest of it is pure, or impure, fiction, indicating a very assured talent.

In a book I just returned to the library I found a marker that illustrates my problem. It's in Alice's hand.

Things not to do

> Tame the wilds
> Break the plains
> Subdue the rivers
> Alter the weather
> Crack the barrier
> Split the atom
> Run, walk, swim, leap
> Faster and higher
> Hit, kick, smash, gouge
> Harder and harder
> Get impatient
> Or expect too much of Kelcey

I must say I find that touching. But without setting myself up as a judge it does seem to me their expectations are unusual. Just this afternoon, making a bank deposit at the drive-up window, my eye was caught by Dahlberg, wearing his helmet, emerging from the lower floor of the shopping plaza on the escalator. It gave me a start. What might they think of next? He crossed the mall at an angle, in his creaky, spread-legged manner, entering the Small World Travel Bureau. This agency features a globe on the roof that revolves. I could see him in the office, leaning on the counter, talking with one of the clerks. Was he planning a space trip or an earth trip? What was I to do? Isn't this expecting too much of Kelcey? With the car behind me honking I had to move. Somehow it put me in mind of how I felt the first time I entered Taubler's apartment. I have yet to tell you about Taubler and Tuchman. On the wall before me he had painted this window, with its view of the sea. A real beach chair was drawn up to face it, the floor around it strewn with the hulls of hand-painted imaginary peanuts.

"He's got his own system," Tuchman said to me, "and you'd better believe it."

Let's say that I've come to believe it. What that still leaves undecided is what I'm to think.

8

ALICE WAS BORN the summer I left college to be a cub reporter for a St. Louis newspaper. Reporters were romantic figures in those days. They went to Russia, to Spain, to Africa, to the dogs. Many prominent writers began as reporters, but most of them proved to have a talent only for beginnings. It's this talent that draws Alice to Dahlberg. I'm not sure what drew her to me, but it's the generation gap that binds us. Puzzlement over my baffling behavior keeps her preoccupied.

But I shouldn't say binds. Alice is not bound. Actually, there is very little mucilage in our natures. In the days of our courtship she liked to read to me from the works of Rilke, a very cagey lover. Binding ties were not his strong points. He spoke of two solitudes that touch, greet, and protect one another. I highly admired the way he put it. Where else but in poetry will lovers find two solitudes appealing? Alice reads very well, with a purr of contentment. Sooner or later Dahlberg will have to face it. One of our neighbor's cats is very fond of me until I scoop her up and try to hold her. Then she goes wild. "Why do you pick her up?" Alice asks me, as she puts iodine on my scratches. I've given it some thought. I persist in feeling (as I did with Alice) that having for long respected her feelings, she might relax and give in to mine. I doubt that she will, but it makes for a lively relationship.

"Where?" she queried, as if puzzled, when I suggested we have a look at Fork River. "Why not, if you'd like to."

We didn't have a perfect day, as I had hoped, the light diffused to a glare by the high overcast, but I wanted to get this visit in while we still had Dahlberg on the payroll. Few things bore Alice more than "going for a ride," but she thought it might do me good to get out of the house and into the open. I was almost sallow. Had I noticed how tanned and healthy Dahlberg looked? Distracted by his sulky manner, and pockmarked features, there were many things I had failed to notice. Had she noticed, I rejoined, that I was a writer, not a house painter? Actually, Alice had something of a tan herself from the time she was now spending in the garden. She wore a wide, floppy-brimmed hat to keep the sun off her face. In the past she had thought it too showy for the natives, but it might be just the thing for Fork River. I loved the gesture, so natural to her, of wiping back the brim with the back of her hand. At the last moment she had decided not to wear the arch-supporting space shoes she had bought just for such an occasion, if one turned up. She wore a sort of ballet slipper that enhanced the slenderness of her feet.

The Big Red had won the game the previous day, so we passed signs of local celebrations, and small fry sporting their red hats and ties. I cannot account for the distaste I feel for small boys dressed up like little men. I had once been one. As I recall I thought very well of myself. I took part in a play where I was henpecked by a wife at least a foot taller, but the funniest lines were mine. The strutting little dictator latent in the male comes out like the first cracked crow of a rooster. Toward little "wives and mothers" I am less venomous, but reserved.

"Are you supposed to be using this road?" Alice said. The high weeds were sweeping the underside of the car.

"It's what Harry and Dahlberg use," I replied, "and it keeps the place private." I wanted to surprise her. My first impression of Fork River had been so special I somewhat feared another. Explorers who came on abandoned cities, or Indian cliff dwellings, must have felt as I did, just for a moment. The time-stopped sensation. The miraculous and unforced overlapping of the past and the present. That it should be right here in the heart of the cornbelt was part of it. The curving road into the canyon seemed worse than I remembered because Alice seemed so apprehensive. It kept her eyes on the road, so that when we made the turn opening out over the river she was not prepared for it.

"Oh my," she said.

"The light's not good at all. When the light is right it's like—" What was it like?

"Who are those people down there?"

On the east side of the river, partially screened by the island willows, we could see a straggly line of hikers, walking along single file. Most of them had green or red packs on their backs. They wore visors or caps.

"They're hikers," I said, "they've hiked in from Bixby. They have a sort of open house on Sundays." Alice had not been prepared for so many other people. She stared at them. "Look up ahead," I said. "Look over there in the clearing." The light was not as crystalline as I had first seen it, but the row of structures, up on piers over the bed of the river, was still hard to believe. Today, however, eight or ten people were seated on the boardwalk, their legs dangling. A few leaned against the buildings, sunning themselves. "What is it?" Alice asked, "a rock concert?"

I'll admit I was not prepared for the hikers. My impression of Fork River—the one I valued—had been of a place empty of people. Others were seated in the sparse shade near the meeting house, eating their packed-in lunches. One small child was running about, spinning like a top. Two cars, one a bright yellow pickup, were parked to get the shade north of the stores. I could see the heat rising off the hood of the pickup. So many people around spoiled it for me.

"Oh, I like it!" Alice said.

I'll admit that surprised me. "I'd like it better without the hippies," I replied. "There wasn't a soul here but the crows and the pigeons."

"I'm not so different," Alice said. "I'm as expectant as they are." She glanced around at them, almost shyly. A few more years made the difference or I would have lost her.

"Harry will like that," I said, and as we moved along the main street I could hear a bell tolling, or rather clanging. A flock of pigeons swooped up from the bell tower and swept low over the treetops, their wings whirring. At the opening of the canyon they careened to the left, spilling their shadows on the hikers, and came back toward the square.

"There's Dahlberg!" Alice cried, and there was Dahlberg opening the doors to the schoolhouse. He was wearing perma-pressed khaki pants and infantry-type boots, with a high polish. He may have seen us approaching, but he moved around with that stiff-jointed solemn caretaker manner he has, his eyes on the ground. His short-sleeved denim shirt was worn with the tails out of the pants. Alice complains if she catches me that way around the house.

"Must be two o'clock," I said, and looked for a shady place to park. I let Alice out, then crossed the wide empty square to a narrow slot of shade at the north end of the buildings. It would get wider as the day lengthened. I left the windows down, and stood there a moment watching the younger people cross toward the schoolhouse. It might have been a scene in a TV movie, stressing ecology and back to the soil. I have admitted to Alice that I regret having missed the tribal reenactment of the sixties. A boy's-life fantasy brought to life, the airways, the freeways, and the sexways open. It boggles the mind. Schoolboys with their knapsacks on the Spanish Steps, at the door to Keats's house. To be a boy for life! Isn't that the American dream? Old enough to shave, to have sex, to vote, but not committed to these options. I think it privately riles Alice that she just missed the early liberated woman pow-wows. She is very assured. They would have loved her. She has the class without the dark glasses. But she is long accustomed to the creature comforts of being a man's wife. Dahlberg had found her. He leaned on the still-polished rail where the departed citizens had once tied up their horses and buggies. His gangly leanness was attractive. He had never smiled for me, but from where I stood, two hundred yards away, I could see the ivory gleam of his teeth. "Ah, well," my Uncle Kermit used to say, ⸻ n the plug from his pipe.

The visitors left their backpacks on ⸻ the schoolhouse, creating a very pretty ⸻ er-hosened German wandervogels u⸻ their blanket rolls on the steps of ⸻ churches with one of their number left to g⸻ them. So it was not so new. Same roles, new faces. As I crossed the square a sudden surge swell of music poured through the doors, like the horn of a speaker. Was it a concert after all? The volume seemed too great for the structure. The pigeons strutting the roof had lifted into the air, as if on the wind of the sound. I had last heard the music in Kansas City, where we had gone to see the movie *2001*. The volume had been about the same, but the circumstances were more auspicious. I seemed to experience the first dawn on the planet. A small group of terrified primates huddled in the shelter of a shallow cave. I saw their terror-stricken eyes. I came very close to feeling as they felt. Not since my childhood had I felt a shudder of awe That awe-filled moment was still in my mind ⸻ n ⸻ ered in bed, hours later.

104

I stood with Alice and Dahlberg, facing the open doors, waiting for the volume of sound to diminish. As the crest passed I said to Dahlberg, "Does it need to be so loud?"

He shrugged. "That's how Harry likes it."

Inside the building I could see that the visitors were taking seats against the walls on cushions. There were no chairs. The light appeared to come through panels in the roof and had a curious subterranean dimness, as if filtered through water. From where I stood the walls appeared to be hung with a series of abstract paintings. Reddish browns, tans, pale greens, electric blues, appeared to be the dominant colors.

"Where's Harry?" I asked.

"Running the show," replied Dahlberg.

"Well, I'm going to catch some of it," I said, and stepped inside. Toward the front of the room, wearing a black cleric's gown, Harry Lorbeer stood with his back to the door, manually operating a slide projector. The screen was centered on the back wall, ten feet above eye level, so that it appeared to be part of the window that opened on the sky. What I had thought to be the moon, seen above the earth's horizon, proved to be the earth just above the moon's horizon. The upper half only was illuminated, so that it resembled the cranium of a human skull. The sensation of space travel was not new, but the experience of unearthly, celestial

105

transport is a matter of imagination. If the astronauts had it, they did not report it.

At two A.M. in the morning, the earth turned from the sun's glare, a simulated TV version of space travel may achieve the appropriate illusions seldom present in a moon landing. I stood gazing at planet earth, floating in space. To grasp it, I must compare it. Is it a blurred cosmic eye, screened by cataracts? Is it a blue and white marble that I once referred to, accurately, as a snotty? But neither cosmic eyes nor marbles bring tremors to the mind's foundations. Off there we are, off there I am, even as I stand on the moon, gazing. My soul is moved in a way that my tongue is unable to record. The hashish eater and the mystic would make the same claim. The view into space is unending, and a measure of man's creative cunning, but the view *from* space compels the awe that will enlarge man's finite nature. It's a brief sensation. The shadow of a bird's flight, and it's gone.

The panels around the walls, taken from satellites in orbit, resembled abstract paintings. I would say it gave the painters some good ideas. The sea was usually jade green, or a deep grotto blue. Deserts were sable tan or reddish-brown, the mountains like the crinkled backs of lizards. Clouds were wide paint smears, or brush splatters, or the pop of aircraft guns. Only the shadows indicated they were not flat on the planet's surface. That thin band of unearthly blue, like a gas flame, was the Valspar skin of air that bathes the globe. There were clouds over Texas and the Gulf, long streaming veils of cirrus, frayed off at the edges. A weather front could be seen to the west, near the Rocky Mountains, a dark crinkle of surface like crumbling blacktop. I could puzzle out the plains thanks to the Missouri, more brown than blue, edging Kansas and Nebraska, with a barely perceptible line showing the Platte River valley. One man-made thing seemed visible. The tiny pimple craters, if you knew where to look, might prove to be football stadiums, where on certain days a mystifying change in the crater's color might be noticed. Of Fork River there was nothing, nor of its mini-crater, nor of Harry Lorbeer's thriving space project, attracting four cars and as many as thirty hikers to share a new experience. The music filled the room like a vapor, in which we were all suspended. After the surfing crest of the opening section there was nowhere for Strauss to go but down. After their long walk some of the guests had dozed off. Harry showed about eight or ten views of the earth from space, climaxed with a full earth view from the moon. Then he switched off the projector but left on the music. His manner was that of a portly, preoccupied priest. The heat of the projector had warmed him up, and he walked through the rear door into the open. I followed him out. We stood together on a porch just high enough to see over the fenced yard, and feel the down-canyon breeze.

"I liked it," I said, "I liked it very much."

He bowed his head slightly, pleased but unsmiling.

"What you're doing here," I said, "is very original. I'd like more people to see it."

He pursed his lips, clasped his hands at the small of his back. In his cleric's gown his bald head and rather long wispy hair seemed part of his costume.

"It's not a matter of numbers, Mr. Kelcey."

"Not to you, but I know many would enjoy it. They are eager to experience this sensation. I could give you the names of people at the National Science Foundation. Dr. Rainey, at the college, should see it."

"There is no time," Harry said flatly. "We go from day to day."

I had almost forgotten he had that obsession. How could a person of such imagination have such childish doubts about the future? What did he fear? The Fork River was just a few miles to the west of the geographic center of the United States, with no visible resources that would lead an enemy to bomb it. We were facing north, up the river ravine, to the mini-crater concealed from our view by the high fence around the play yard, or whatever it was. It had been raked smooth as sandpaper, strewn with a few dead leaves. I thought I would work up to the crater, by degrees.

"I like this," I said, gesturing over the fence, "whatever it is, it seems to promise something." He made no comment. "Is it for something?"

"For something? It's for *them.*"

"Them who?" A mistake the moment I said it. Harry's solemn, widely spaced eyes looked over my face piecemeal, seeking a clue to my ignorance.

"Them, *them!*" he said, waving both hands at the sky. "It's for them, whoever they are."

"A place to land?" I said.

"A place to land." That pleased him. He felt somewhat reassured about me.

"You can't believe that," I said.

"What do you mean, I can't believe it? I *can* believe it. It's you that *can't* believe it."

Men of Harry Lorbeer's type are not humorists. I will go farther and say that a sense of humor shows a deficiency of faith in oneself, as well as others. If I were a true believer, I wouldn't smile. Through Harry Lorbeer I have come to question many things I took for granted. When you hear somebody say, "That's only human," be on your guard. If I had faith the size of a mustard seed I would arrange my affairs, close up the house, send Alice home to her mother, and stand here on the porch of Harry Lorbeer's chapel with my eyes on the sky. But I am deficient in faith. The glittering saucer-shaped object will prove to be on the ball of my eye.

"You're right, Harry," I said. "I don't believe it. I've got some kind of block when it comes to believing. I can accept anything after it happens, but less and less, so to speak, on credit. Why is that? I don't like what it implies."

"You better believe it," said Harry, "or it's not going to happen."

He did not say what, but it struck me as true. The fact that I'd better believe it. Why is it that people totally lacking in humor arouse in us feelings of compassion? *They* had all the fun. What was there to pity them for? I put my hand, briefly, on Harry's shoulder in puzzled, troubled good-fellowship. He did not seem to mind. I felt that what we both missed in life was a younger or older person to lean on. In the room at our back Strauss and Zarathustra were building to another climax. If anything was going to happen the time was ripe.

"They come in from the west," Harry said, "you know, with the airflow, with the planet's rotation." He put his finger out and made a stirring motion, glanced at me to see if I was with him. I was, all the way. On the veined lids of my eyes I saw the swirling globe gather into its vortex assorted, nameless flying objects, some unidentified. "But not to take off," he continued, "takeoffs are counter clockwise."

"Of course," I said. We both saw them, through a giddy swirl of air, and soft humming top music, take off against the planet's rotation.

"It's *unconventional,* Kelcey, but it's not unusual." In his eyes I saw the expectancy of my father, holding the string on which the gyroscope twirled, like a dancer. "God dammit, boy," he said, "never mind *why,* the point is it works."

Alice and Dahlberg, Alice holding some tall weeds and seed pods for a dried arrangement, came down the path from the mini-crater, but it did not seem to have impressed her. Quite the contrary. She looked as she did when coming into the house from her own garden, her arms full of flowers. I noticed again that Dahlberg—young as he was— seemed to find the manners of his elders congenial, his hands at the small of his back, the left wrist gripped firmly by the right hand. Did I detect in him the tendency to combine the mature and the youthful?

"There's Alice," I said, "she probably wants to get back. We've had a wonderful time. Can we come again?" Harry bowed slightly, a solemn guru. If I *was* a believer in the shots from space, better not to admit it, and keep him waiting. His belief would be larger. It would make my belief a childish thing.

"Harry," I said, "what if I come out on a weekday? I'd like to just sit here. We could skip the music. It might do something for my character."

Such a remark was lost on Harry: or maybe it was *not* lost on him. I saw that he believed it. His head nodded.

"See Mr. Lindner," he said, "he will let you in."

I thanked him and went to look for Alice. The steps at the front were now in the shade, and Alice was seated on the low one, toying with her dried arrangements. Dahlberg leaned on the hitchbar. The music pouring out of the open doors made it hard to talk.

"Did you see the hole?" I asked. "Isn't that something?"

As I suspected, it did not have much impact on Alice. Both Dahlberg's boots and her yellow slippers were coated with a film of dust. Alice's forehead showed the first touches of the prickly heat that enhances her complexion. The lobes of her ears were translucent.

"I think we better get back," I said, and she seemed willing. Dahlberg sauntered along with us, in his gangly way, to where the car was parked in the shade of the buildings. Another car was there, with an out-of-state license. If this kept up they would have a winner. How would they handle that?

"We'll be back," I said. With Alice there he didn't make his usual comment. Neither did I slip up and say, "See you tomorrow." He seemed even less inclined to talk than usual, and we drove off without the usual banter. A few new arrivals were straggling in from the south, some of them wading in the shallow water. Even the willows on the islands looked hot and dusty. "I'm glad we don't have to face that walk back," I said.

Alice seemed preoccupied. A woman seated, absently holding flowers, especially a dried arrangement, has something sadly wistful about her. The flowers suggest losses, illusions. There were many things I meant to tell her but I hesitated to intrude on her mood. She was in a "study," a word her mother often used. Out on the highway, I said, "A penny for your thoughts," usually good for a smile.

"When I asked him what he wanted to do, you know what he said?"

I did not.

"He said, *I want to restore awe.* Just like that. I just can't explain why it moved me. He has a deep religious streak in his nature."

"I know," I replied, "not everybody feels that life is a hoax." Again a mistake. I should have suppressed it, but she hardly seemed to have heard me.

"He said that without awe we diminish, we trivialize, everything we touch."

Something childlike in her acceptance was touching. I had the good sense to keep my mouth shut. I had meant to tell her about my talk with Harry, and his landing site for the UFOs. "You'd *better* believe it," I was going to tell her, and laugh, but I knew she wouldn't believe it. She would merely think that I was silly enough to try to discredit Dahlberg. If there had been less rudeness in his nature I would have liked him better. Trivialize is one of my favorite verbs.

9

I AWOKE to see the light on the shrubs and trees near the deck. Alice had smoothed back the covers, but her side of the bed was cold. She likes to read cookbooks if she can't sleep, topping the night off with a pre-dawn gourmet breakfast. She'll get back to bed at about the time our neighbors are getting up. The Fitches are good neighbors, as they remind us at Christmas, with a UNICEF card signed by their five children, all but the last child, a slip-up, sensibly staggered at two-year intervals. The last child, Rodney, came six years after his sister, Charlotte. With the appearance of Rodney the first four children became aware of what they had in common. They were the in-group. Rodney was the out. I catch him spying on me through the slats of their porch, where he likes to sit with one of his pet chickens. The Fitches are aware of Rodney's problem, and he has things of his own, like chickens. The Fitch dog, Elmo, belongs to them all, but he spends most of his time in the station wagon, doing chores and errands with Mrs. Fitch. Mr. Fitch is a GO BIG RED man who likes to power-mow his lawn early Sunday morning and play with a snow scooter in the winter. Since the third Fitch child, Clarence, they leave the house for school in the morning passing just below our bedroom window. Mrs. Fitch comes to the door to see them off. "Bye now," she says. "Bye now," they reply. "Bye now," she repeats. The older children now take off on bikes, but Rodney maintains this tradition. I've noticed that Alice hasn't managed to feel for him as she should.

If I wake up at night I have trouble accepting the world. Darkness conceals it, as it once concealed the face of the deep. What I know to be real seems so unreal I put my hands to my face, covering my eyes. A strange gesture. I do it to see more, as well as less. What I seem to see best is mirrored on the balls of my eyes. In the last few weeks, few nights, it's been the earth in space. There it floats, vapors swirl about it, or I see it like a skull on the moon's horizon. They tell me that the wall of China is the only man-made thing that is visible. Those chaps looking at it from Mars would think it a canal. Knowing what it is, we grasp what we dimly see. If I then zoom in on points of interest to me, the patchy continent of Europe, or parts of North America, I experience a pleasurable quandry. I see *where* it is—France, the oceans, and the plains—but I do not see *when* it is. That's my own talent, or my own weakness. In my boyhood my father took me to the Rockies, where he had a cabin in Estes Park. Of all that I recall little or nothing. My memory is blocked by a single vibrant image, of the great plains spreading eastward from the mountains. I saw it from a train window. In a way, it was my first view from space. The plains fell away eastward in a manner that left me dizzy, as if the earth were spinning. My father pointed out to me that the wisp of smoke, far away and below us, was a train approaching. I strained to see it, but I saw nothing moving. How could he speak of it as approaching? "It's not moving," I said, or something like that, and he explained that was due to the distance. If one was far enough from what was moving, the movement seemed to stop. Sometime later we passed this train thundering past us in the opposite direction. What could my father have meant? How did distance bring a rushing train to a stop?

If we are a few hundred miles in space, nothing visibly moves on the surface of the planet. Like shadows, we see that they move when we turn away. If one carried this impression to its conclusion, apparent movement would cease, apparent time would stop, at some point in space. From some point in space, that is, given the view, I might zoom in and see a huge leaf-eating monster, foraging in the swampy ravine of the Fork River. From another point I would zoom in and find it all covered with ice. In the full light of day, of course, I doubt that, I make a clear distinction between fact and fiction, but in the full bloom of night I zoom down to watch the Druids dragging their slabs of rock to Stonehenge. They wear pelts, but otherwise they look like a typical crowd at a football rally. Dahlberg is there. Harry Lorbeer is there. And I am there at the fringe of the circle, gawking. Alice cowers with other womenfolk around the fire. If we get over this idea of looking backwards, we will note fewer backward characteristics. These people were shorter, but otherwise the same as those assembled at Fork River on Sunday. They loved mystery. They looked with wonder at the sky. Among them was a man, a true believer, whose mind buzzed with nameless unidentified flying objects, requiring only the right incantation to bring down what was up, and lift up what was down. He wore a blackish pelt, a solemn air, and he was free of the frailty of humor.

I suppose it's the bleakness of this scene I like, perpetually bathed in a lunar twilight. I know the sun shines on Stonehenge, but not in my mind. Far off the sun either sets or it rises, and they are of two minds about it. What a sensation! Hooded with night, on whose authority could they assume the sun would rise? That's what moves me. Waiting for dawn after such a doubt. It's this surging, miraculous dawn that I hear in Strauss's music, and the terror and mystery of it that I saw in the cowering primates. Somewhere on the planet, according to my theory, they are huddled in a cave's mouth as dawn approaches. Light is a physical presence that overpowers darkness. The terror they feel makes them a single creature. They cling to each other as to their mother. If I zoom in on them, however, my compassion gives way to pity. The poor dumb brutes! Thank God they do not know what lies ahead. This pity, in turn, is diminished by the knowledge of my own ignorance. I know as little of what lies ahead as the apes. I turn away from this scene to another where a fire burns at a cave's entrance. How this fire attracts me, clearing a small space in the dark! I feel its warmth, by the flicker of its flames I see the figures huddled about it. They are past merely cowering. The terror they feel lifts the hair on their limbs, as it widens their eyes. I recognize Harry Lorbeer, wearing a deerskin and a fur cap that makes him look very Russian, with his widely spaced eyes. He is not so frightened as puzzled at what he sees before him. He has a stick with a rattle on its tip that he rattles. More practical, the woman seated on his left throws wood on the fire. The flames light up the cave interior and on the wall at the back, along with his shadow, I see the gangly gawky figure of Dahlberg, daubing at the wall with a rounded stick. He is tracing the outline of a creature, one of many that charge across the wall's face. I see they are bisons. The flickering of the light enhances the impression of their movement. Suddenly the figure turns, feeling my gaze, and gives me a wild, hostile stare. His hair stands up around his head. The fire burns on his eyes. This fellow is possessed. He holds his paint-daubed stick like a club. At his side, crouching, in a fawn-colored pelt that goes very well with her eyes and complexion, I recognize Alice. She is stirring up a mixture of fresh colors. She prefers this more creative-type work to cutting up the fresh kill, or tending the fire. Glancing up, as if she heard me speak, I see that she feels a certain pity for me, a man too old to hunt.

In spite of the fur pelts they wear, and the dark, smoke-filled cave, reeking of the odors of burned flesh and dung heaps, I recognize these people as my friends playing their roles. There is a child howling somewhere in the exact tones of Rodney Fitch. There has to be a dog, but he is probably back in the shadows, asleep. As strange and as familiar as I find this scene, what I like is the sense of something dawning. They have the faith, and you'd better believe it! It will of course take some doing, but they are working at it. That woman stirring the pot has things on her mind. Sunset is surely a worrisome time for people who have no reason to believe there will always be a sunrise—and that's where belief came in. They needed that assurance, and they got it. Here's the way it all works, one of them said, and that was how it was.

Now if we zoom in on a point we refer to as later, just west of the Missouri River, some time following the Ice Age, we will find Harry Lorbeer a keeper of the faith in his off hours as a handyman and plumber. He's got a flock, of sorts, he's got a high priest, and he's got a dawn-plan for the future, the eternal reenactment of flying objects, unidentified. Lying there in the dark, I'm obliged to tell you, my heart belongs to Harry. It's a game of dawnings. We're all Stonehenge hunters at heart. To feel we are in on the dawn of something is a pitiful, shameful, humiliating illusion, which you can see in the eyes of most of the respectable people you know. The things that they believe! My God, it would break the heart. But what we see in the eyes of the nonbelievers is even more disconcerting. It has been described. It is what we call the status quo. Thinking of it I felt a surge of warm fellow feeling for Dahlberg. He was no fool. He couldn't look me in the eye and tell me that he was a licensed flying saucer pilot. For that he needed Alice's eyes. I thought about him with sympathy, in this context, and regretted that I had been so peevish. I got up to see what time it was, and perhaps say something reassuring to Alice. They were young. What could they do with their feelings but have them?

By the clock in the hall it was five past four, not so late as I had thought. Alice was seated with her feet curled up beneath her, on the couch, but she was not reading. She had a pad in her lap, but the reading lamp was turned to shine through the window on the deck and the bushes. I could see she was doodling with a red felt-tip pen. Alice's doodles are small button-size creatures with shell-like whorls that go round and round. They looked to me like mini-traps. She was so preoccupied I couldn't tell if I was being ignored, or she hadn't heard me. "The Birkins leave a light on in their kitchen," I said, "have you noticed that?"

In her minor depressions Alice will doodle to avoid a tantrum or my conversation. I could see that she was doodling with the felt-tip pen she had given me for Christmas. "Why are things as they are?" she said.

You know, that surprised me. Simple-minded questions are often unnerving. For too many years I had seldom thought of H. Taubler. Now I thought of him. I said, "Are *what?*" Then I said, "We're all Chicken Littles. We can't kick the habit. Suppose you got up in the morning and found the furniture attached to the ceiling?"

"What a ridiculous idea."

"It has its appeal," I said, "it breaks the habit. By

now I would say Taubler would have tried it. He was wild. He stood things on their heads. He painted himself into, then out of Paris. You keep at something like that long enough and one day things are no longer what they were."

"Who was Taubler?"

I shrugged. "I don't think he knew. He was still working at it." I could see that she was thinking of Dahlberg. "One thing I can tell you, Alice," I said, "don't look at anything too closely." She looked at me very closely. "Take the UFOs. You know when the jig is up? The jig is up as soon as one is identified."

I could see that didn't help much. I stooped to scratch at a spot on the rug. Was it fresh paint?

Foolishly I asked her, "What have you been reading?"

"Intellectuals are like a can of worms without dirt," she replied.

If there is something to be said for the young, is it picturesque speech? I used to fork up worms and store them in fruit jars, just for the hell of it. If I went fishing I put them in a can I carried by the lid. Not knowing the head of the worm from the tail I found it hard to slip them onto the hook.

I walked into the kitchen and switched off the night light, opening the drapes. The dawn was colorless as water. I felt the chill of those primates eternally huddled at the cave's mouth. Above the trees the sky was streaked with traveling light. All I need to see is something like that to know that dawn's chariot is approaching, hitched up to white horses with flowing manes. Growing up and growing old have not diminished that impression. The same flood of light washed me into space where I weightlessly tumbled in orbit. I saw the surface of the earth curve out of darkness into daylight, and then out of daylight into darkness. At the point where the light and the dark commingled, over Fork River, Kansas, I saw myself. The immense pathos of my situation was part of the cosmic perspective, as if I shared with the cosmos the vast indifference of the prime mover. In this way, momentarily, I had learned to live with things as they are.

"I'm going to scramble us some eggs," I said, and stood for a moment in the draft from the refrigerator, the chill, impersonal winds of space blowing into my face.

IO

IN THE LAST FEW WEEKS, passing the new shopping plaza, I speculate on how it must look from space. More than five hundred acres of blacktop parking. In the early morning hardly a car in sight, just the blackboard surface with the cross-hatched white lines in a bold hound's-tooth pattern. As the day progresses the cross-hatching disappears and you would see gleaming, metallic, checkered colors, with dazzling jewel-like reflections. What would an orbiting spaceman make out of it? A spacewoman might see a garden, blossoming in the sunlight. A spacespy would see a changing, coded message. Alice would see that she needed new glasses.

Directly across from the plaza is Burke's Salvage

Emporium, an eyesore collection of war surplus quonset huts. In with the battered pickups and shiny hotrods I saw the VW van with the metal ladders on the top. I didn't think it would be Harry's van, but it was, both sides daubed with faded green and yellow flowers. Had Dahlberg run out of paint? It seemed early in the day for him to have stopped. Along with paint, Burke's sold at a discount everything any of us will need when it's too late. Flying suits, sleeping bags, rubber blankets, inflatable rafts, rope hammocks, plastic canoes, wind gauges, path finders, height estimators, fallout helmets and goggles, shovels, guns and ammunition, pocket warmers, food cookers, tents, balloons, pith helmets, hunting knives, canned water, dehydrated food, snake bite and survival kits, vitamins and water purifiers. I browse in Burke's while Alice does the shopping. I could see how it might appeal to Dahlberg. A few years back I bought a war surplus field scope, but without the directions as to how to use it, or what it was for. I thought it might be a good time to ask Dahlberg about it.

I parked in the gravel at the back and went in under a ceiling of inflated rubber rafts, between racks of second-hand flyers' uniforms. It was easy to pick out the flyers that were not so lucky. Why did the uniforms look so familiar? It was the outfit Dahlberg wore to paint in. I saw him soon enough, his copper hair glistening under one of the domed ceiling skylights. He had one eye closed; through the other he squinted through the eyepiece of an instrument used by navigators to determine their position at sea. He looked great. One of those dauntless Swedes who are born and bred to explore something. The instrument he was sighting through, or trying to, was an astrolabe. High racks of secondhand clothes, jackets, and flight suits concealed the shorter person who stood beside him. I assumed it was Harry. A gleaming orange helmet sat on his head. People of the sort of Dahlberg and Harry, as well as certain types of men in general, have a weakness for war salvage, especially if it's of a mechanical nature. I have a telescope myself, along with its tripod, which proves to be so heavy I seldom use it, but once I saw it I couldn't do without it. The whole setup came in a heavy wooden case that we now use for storage in the basement. It cost the government $700. It cost me $39.95, plus freightage. So I was not so surprised at what I saw as curious. What the hell did he expect to do with an astrolabe? Ignorance as to how to use one, or what it was for, had always prevented me taking the leap. We have plenty of stars in Nebraska, but no pressing need for instrument navigation.

Now and then the person concealed by the clothes racks thrust an arm into the air and wriggled it through the sleeve of a heavy quilted jacket, electric blue in color, puffed up with insulation like a flight suit. Farmers out here wear them in the winter. People are no longer so fussy about how they look. I could see the way Dahlberg wagged his head he needed time to make up his mind. He's like a kid. He shifts from foot to foot, rubs his hand over his head. Alice likes that. It's the child in him she likes. Astrolabes are not cheap, however, and a house painter has little need of one. He helped Harry out of the jacket he had managed to get on, then lifted off the helmet, fluffing out the hair that stood around his head like a halo. Understandably it reminded me of Alice. It was her hair. She tipped back her head to look up at Dahlberg, and the exertion had heightened her color. She looked excited and pleased. I would almost say she looked as thrilled as a kid. Of course she had to have a look through the astrolabe, where she saw nothing but her lashes. What was it for? He patiently explained, gazing into the darker regions of the ceiling. To be perfectly frank, the pair of them belonged on the recruiting posters you see in post office lobbies. They were in orbit. They were where everybody wanted to be. The astrolabe also came with a leather case that he explained was worth the price by itself. Did he want it? Then he must have it. Her head dropped from sight as she scrounged in her purse. Dahlberg held off for several agonizing moments, dipping and wagging his head as if in pain, then he gave in. He carried the helmet and the astrolabe toward the cashier at the front end. I couldn't see much of Alice, but I think she went along carrying the quilted jacket. What were they up to? I didn't have time to think. I went out through the rear door I had come in, and moved the car to the back of the parking lot. We drive a Plymouth. Alice often forgets what it looks like when she goes shopping. I have to taxi over and look for it in the parking lot. They got into Dahlberg's van, where they had a discussion (I could see his big head wagging), then they drove out on the highway and headed east. You won't believe this, but I just sat there in the car. I didn't think about much. It did cross my mind that some predicaments lie out of the range of urgent decisions, such as the purchase and use of an astrolabe. Was I in shock? I could watch the hands move on the clock in the Fairview Shopping Center. When it was time for me to go home, that was where I went. Dahlberg's van was parked in the street, and one of his shorter ladders leaned on the house wall, his paint-smeared shoes at its foot. When I pulled into the driveway I saw them on the deck. Alice waved.

"Dahlberg took me shopping!" she called. "Wasn't that nice?" She stood up to look at me through her new cheap war surplus bird glasses. Not liking what she saw, she tried looking at me through the wrong end. "You look far away!"

she cried, waving. Was I wrong in thinking that she liked that better? Slouched in one of the deck chairs Dahlberg held up his glass, rocking the ice cubes.

II

It's a new age. I've written about it myself. People —women especially—are free to lead their own lives, and I am all for it. Alice has often heard me say so. As I would not be a slave, I told her, neither would I be a master. She appreciates the lessons of the past applied to the present. My own opinion hasn't changed, but my interest has grown in the life she might be leading. I said, "I'm going to run over and see Miss Ingalls—"

"You can take that last book back," she replied. She was out in the garden, with her new bird glasses. Dahlberg was up on the ladder, working under the eaves. He is careless about the paint that he drips on the driveway, but a non-drip painter is a slow worker. The book to go back to the library was a collection of Arthur C. Clarke's science fiction. Just a few weeks back Alice would have burned it rather than admit she had read it. But as I keep telling myself, it's her own life. She had left a card in the book as a marker, with a few words scribbled on it. "The moon is our first bridgehead into space." If I had said that in my sleep she would have been on the phone to her doctor. Who is *our?* I leaned out of the car to call to her that I might not make it back for lunch. I'm a talented fibber, but it's not easy for me to tell a lie. I had said I was going to the library to see Miss Ingalls, so that was where I went. I saw her, checking books at the desk, dropped off the one I had brought, then left. It seemed reasonable to me that Alice, to save Dahlberg the money, would give him his lunch. If I did not come back for lunch, they would both take off. I parked near the intersection of the east-west highway with our own street, Sunset Terrace, in the shade of a billboard advertising the State Fair. I've always made it a point to take Alice to the Fair. To smell real manure, hear chickens cackle, and put your hand for a furtive, incredible moment on the moist snout of a calf, or the rump of a hog, is a very earthy experience. Alice had been a forest creature, not a farmer, but she liked to put in a day at the Fair. We had been so preoccupied with Harry and Dahlberg we had both forgotten about it. The billboard assured me that it still had three days to go. The thing for me to do—I didn't have to think about it, it occurred to me as a package—was ask them both if they wouldn't like to take a little time off. That would surprise them. I could appreciate the effort it would cost Alice not to exchange glances with Dahlberg. In little surprises I hoped to maintain the initiative.

As peculiar as I personally found Dahlberg, with his facial tics and mannerisms, it was possible for me to understand that a girl like Alice might be drawn to him. I don't confuse that with the usual attractions. *Drawn* is what water does to divining rods. Grown-up boys will sometimes have a greater *draw* than male grown-ups. At ten minutes to one, sooner than I expected, I saw the van approaching me from the south, the driver wearing a sunflower yellow crash helmet. Glare off the windshield concealed his companion. Trailing them, with several cars between us, I realized how many movies and TV thrillers relied on vans to get the dirty work done. You can't see into a van. Nothing looks so ordinary from the outside. Just as an example, they could have in it, for a quick getaway, one of those two-seater motorbikes. In the big vans they store cars. I've seen it in the movies. While they are cruising along, with an escort of cops, they paint the whole shebang and change the motor serial number. With a little imagination there are a lot of uses for a van.

To avoid the downtown traffic they turned north, then west again near the Aggie campus. Between the scattered houses and leafless trees I could see the bright arc of a ferris wheel, with its rocking gondolas. We have a great State Fair, acres and acres of cows, pigs, chickens, and horses. Alice is scared of hogs, but she likes them. Nothing else so big is so graceful on such small pins. Has your attention ever been called to the eyes of a sow? Her lashes are long. She favors the languorous, lidded gaze. A sow with a litter of piglets at her teats, snorting little snorts of pleasure, may well change your mind about pork chops. I owe all of that to Alice, but last year, unfortunately, she found that some creatures who won the prizes were marched or dragged off to the slaughter. Had it been Dahlberg's idea to take her to the Fair? That's where we were headed, and it was too late for me to turn back. Up ahead of me thousands of cars were parked in fields of corn stubble, looking like they lacked wheels. I lost track of the van while I was parking, then I spotted the pair of them, their helmets gleaming, walking along hand-in-hand like a pair of knighted hippies. Until that moment I had failed to grasp their strategy. Who would ever recognize them in such outfits? Her helmet was white, with a sea-green visor, the electric blue quilted jacket puffed her out like a kewpie. Naturally they were headed for the livestock exhibits, but it seemed to me that Dahlberg kept her moving. Alice liked to put her hand on the moist snout of a calf, and smell her milky breath. In a pen freshly spread with straw I saw this gangly farm kid, lean as a puppet, sprawled as if he had been tossed there in his sleep. Seated on a bale of hay, his straw hat tipped back, a cowhand with short, rope-polished fingers peeled off a cigarette paper, shaped it to a trough, then tapped the tobacco from a pouch of Bull Durham. A farmboy watched him, his jaw slack, a green wad of blowgum locking his teeth. Neither gave me a glance. A cream-colored calf gazed in my direction but gave no indication that he saw me, an object in space he felt no need to identify.

Had I lost them? The racket of the music and hawkers was deafening, but on a weekday afternoon there were few people. Most of the rides sat idle. One in operation was like a huge auger stretched out on its side, boring a hole in space. The cars followed the circling curve of the bit, doing the loop-the-loop. A ride like that scares me to death. Adjoining the loop-the-loop, and not a ride at all, as far as I could determine, two steel columns supported an object resembling a motorcycle sidecar. From another angle it might be taken as a car hoist, or a cement mixer. The sidecar had a snapdown lid with a strip of green plastic as a cover. In a prison camp or a war movie it might be taken as a device of torture. A steep flight of stairs connected the car with the ground. At the foot of the stairs, on a low platform, a chap wearing a cap with a duckbill visor sat smoking a cigar and reading a newspaper. The operator—if that was what he was—was like a businessman at a coffee break. People in his line of work interested me. What is it like, day after day, to sell a life of thrills and gaiety? He looked like a car mechanic. Did he swap joy rides with his colleagues? Somewhere—my guess would be Oklahoma or Texas—he had a wife at home watching TV and several hoodlum-type kids resisting the powers of education. Chances are they had never found the time, nor the money, to enjoy the thrills sold by daddy. When they were asked what their daddy did, what did they say? On the platform at his side was a megaphone wired to an amplifier. Shouting was pointless. He had to broadcast to be heard. How people in his line of work must hate the slow-witted, tight-fisted yokel who would not part with his money just to have a good time. The ride was short and sweet, but life was long. Mechanical constructions designed for pleasure have a special melancholy when they are idle. Especially merry-go-rounds. It occurred to me that these new monstrous rides were like objects fallen from space and wrecked. I wondered if Harry had thought of that. Or was Dahlberg the one who liked to speculate? The loop-the-looping cars, called the SCREWDRIVER, had pulled in and stopped but the two passengers just sat there. They wore helmets, and looked like Mamma and Papa bugs. Were they stunned, or merely dazed? The operator had to lean over and shout at Dahlberg. That seemed to revive him, he squirmed in the seat, then wriggled to where he could squeeze a hand into his pocket. What did he want? He wanted the fare for another ride. It was not a long one, maybe seven or eight loops, but I could see that two rides were enough. They needed a little help getting out of the cab, and recovering what we call our balance. I had observed this in returning astronauts. They left the SCREWDRIVER, stood for a moment feeling the good solid earth beneath them, then proceeded directly to the object I have described. The operator explained that only one person could ride at a time. There was a brief discussion between Alice and Dahlberg, with Dahlberg conceding that ladies went first. She went up the ladder to the cockpit, and the operator went up to buckle her in, check her out. Dahlberg stepped back from the apparatus to watch her take off. What it proved to be was one of these flight simulators that puts you through the full works of flying: over and over, tilts and dips, with a few of the drops you get in elevators. Not long. Although it seemed long to me, the lady being my wife. He let her sit there for a moment to recover or scream, then he went up and opened the hatch. They had a brief discussion, but she seemed to be all right. The operator helped her down, then he was thoughtful enough to let her sit in his chair while Dahlberg went into orbit. My visceral feelings were that the shorter person had the better chance. A tall gangly test tube, like Dahlberg, had too great a gap between his head and his feet. What if the fluids of the inner ear slipped out of place? Alice had opened her visor to get a breath of fresh air, but I could not see her face. While Dahlberg was dipping and tilting in orbit I took off.

I hurried back through the stock barns (the boy in the hog pen still drugged with sleep, sprawled on the straw) then across the fields to my car, the windshield waxed by a Halloween prankster. I drove to a diner near the airport where I sipped coffee and watched the planes glide in and roar out. It's not what you know that proves to be the problem, but what you admit. A farmboy could have seen what I had seen and drawn the sensible, obvious conclusion. Some people are determined to get into orbit. Was it so unusual that one of them was my wife?

On my way home I stopped at the market for a six-pack of High Life, Dahlberg's beer, and a bottle of Wolfschmidt's vodka. Alice liked gin for standing-up drinking, vodka for sitting down.

"You just missed him," Alice said, putting ice in the glasses. "He put in a long day—how was yours?"

How slender she looked! I would say the flight training had done wonders for her circulation. A glow to her cheeks, but a palpable tremor to her drinking hand.

"There's a fair on," I said, "would you like to go?"

She pretended not to hear me.

"You're going to miss him," I said, "aren't you?"

"You're shouting," she replied, "why are you shouting?"

I suppose I was compensating, as we say, trying to get through. Weightless in space, do we have communication problems?

"Cheers!" I said, hoisting my glass, and glanced up to see a reflection in the deck window that surprised me. It proved to be myself.

12

WHEN I CAME OUT OF MY STUDY the door to the
bathroom stood ajar, the mirror reflecting a corner
of the living room and the deck. They were out on
the deck, standing at the rail. Dahlberg had placed
both hands on Alice's shoulders and held her off at
arm's length, like a framed painting. There was
something so solemn, so ceremonial, about it, I was
neither startled nor offended. Her face tilted upward, as I had often seen it, radiant with expectations. If one view of Dahlberg is better than another, it's the one from below. If he had sprinkled
her with water it would not have surprised me. She
wore a caftan that hung to her ankles, and looked

like a child home from communion. Rather than spy on such a moment I backed off.

A moment later I heard them talking in their usual carefree manner and joined them. Slouched in one of the deck chairs, Dahlberg was saying that the way to change the world was to change one's perspective. No one should see it up close: even the man who made it. It should look like what it was, not what it had become. One should see it in space, round and luminous as a lantern, with swirling clouds that both concealed and revealed it. Inside its film of air it would float like a cosmic eye. When the time came to launch the first landing party, they should collect only soil, beer, and peanut butter. No people. People were the contaminators. There should be a new way of breeding people, like in eggs. He personally felt that the egg was the perfect solution since nobody could determine which came first.

It was quite a little sermon he delivered, and not the first time Alice had heard it. She amused herself fishing for a cube of ice. In a casual, passing-the-time sort of manner I asked him where he planned to go on his trip. I may have said *drip*, an understandable slip. We once had a guest drop into one of our sling chairs the moment after the neighbor's cat had left a puddle. He wore the same expression as Dahlberg. Just a few expressions have to serve for countless circumstances. Alice sat with a cube of ice clamped in her mouth.

"I just happened to be passing Small World," I said. "You know, the agency. Saw you through the window."

Alice spit up her ice cube, said, "Oh, that was for me. He was asking for me."

"You're taking a trip?"

More toying with the ice cube. "I was thinking maybe *we* might, after New Year's. You're always complaining about the long winters."

"I complain," I said, "but I don't plan to move. It's cold here, but nobody's shooting at us. What place you have in mind?"

Dahlberg said, "The Bahamas, Guatemala, Honolulu—" He sounded like an airport plane caller.

"All he was doing was *asking,"* said Alice. "If there was something special we were going to surprise you."

"Oh, boy!" I chortled. I simply couldn't help it. A single glance passed between us like a pool shot. How avoid implicating remarks? "Alice knows I don't fly," I said, making it worse, and leaned forward to stuff my mouth with Fritos. I felt terrible. The salt on the Fritos burned my lips. "God knows, Alice—" I said, "you're free to take a trip anywhere you'd like to. Guatemala, Honolulu, the moon, or wherever—" There's no stopping something like

142

that once you start it. I suddenly popped up, said, "I feel like some music. Any requests?" There were no requests. I hustled inside, dusting the salt from my hands, and made a to-do of looking through the record albums. They sat like the lovers in a Bergman movie. I picked Benny Goodman's *Sing, Sing, Sing,* turned up the volume on Krupa's drumming. Alice went to the bathroom for a few minutes, leaving Dahlberg on the deck, rocking his beer can. People are crazy. If we admit to that, we can do pretty well. Alice and I danced a bit to the "5 o'clock Stomp," then we both stepped out on the deck to cool off. She looked radiant. How I look is well known.

"You were great," said Dahlberg. I think he meant it.

"We used to cut a bit of rug in the old days," I said.

"Oh they were not so old," said Alice.

"You know what," I said, "I'm going to take the Fifth Amendment." That broke it up. We all shared a common fit of laughter, and when it passed the music had stopped. I went to the kitchen for some more cold beer. When I came back Alice was studying Dahlberg through the wrong end of her new bird glasses. Was that the new perspective that he had recommended? she asked. It made him look far away. It pleased me to detect in Dahlberg's quick glance that the feminine mystique was a shared problem. Woman would be the same, no matter from where we saw her. In spite of Dahlberg's high-pitched, almost squeaky, voice, he had an appealing, mocking way of humoring himself. Now and then he wagged his head as if to free it from cobwebs. In a small, private fit of wheezing laughter he sucked air through his teeth, making a noise like a siphon. In the dappled shade of our open deck he looked mature and melancholy, having lost a little weight. I felt a twinge of concern about his health. Was he getting enough sleep? I don't think he would have minded if I had asked him, directly, if he anticipated certain navigation problems, but in the perspective I had at the moment it seemed a matter of little interest. We were all navigators. We did what we could with whatever we had.

Without warning Alice said, "Read him your poem, read him your poem!" A sure sign of her excitement was the way she failed to show it. Dahlberg looked stunned. God knows, I knew how he felt. This was something strictly between them. Why in heaven's name did she want me to hear it?

"If you won't, I *will,*" she said, pushed up out of her chair, and stomped off the deck. Dahlberg sat with his head tilted back, as if gazing, dumbstruck, into space. His jaw was slack. He couldn't seem to believe what it was he saw. Alice was back in an instant with a piece of cream-colored deckle-edged paper. It appeared to be written in some sort of script, with flourishes. "You won't read it?" she asked.

He was speechless.

"Then I will," she said, and read it. The one clear impression I had was that it was not for the first time.

Some creatures are fierce, others are gentle, still others have remarkably peculiar customs, including birds of the air, fish of the sea, and animals that read newspapers.

When I read that Africa is rich in diamonds, Arabia is rich in oil, the seas are rich in minerals and America is rich in gold, I know that people are crazy.

On a recent night, sleeping fitfully, I heard the earth crack along one of its seams like an apple . . . Soon I will hear it again. The sound goes on and on, like the ringing of an axe in the forest.

Creatures are various, some of them foolish, and the earth floats like a skull above the moon's horizon, almost within our reach.

"Hey, that's good," I said. "That's really good."

"I forgot to read the title," said Alice. "It's *Coda.*"

"It sounds great," I went on, "but I suspect it *reads* better. You've got a lot of meat in it. I'd like to read it."

"Somebody's *got* to publish it," said Alice. She gave me the first direct look I had had in weeks. An appealing look. I mean a look full of appeal.

"Of course," I said. "If you'd like me to I can

mention it to this fellow at Harper's. We've had some correspondence. He likes me to keep him in mind."

One of the big jays that daily raids our feedbox swooped in like a falcon, scattering birdseed. Dahlberg leaped up to flail his arms in a surprisingly aggressive manner. Was this the man of peace, including birds of the air, or a mere reader of newspapers? The people we are comfortable with are fictions: if the real person speaks up we're shocked.

"I don't know about you two," Alice said, "but I feel like a *real* drink," and left us to make one.

Leaning on the deck rail, gazing across the plains to the south, Dahlberg said, "You know, Kelcey, I'm going to miss it."

I'm not going to say more than tell you quite simply what it was he said.

13

WE HAD DAHLBERG for two days, working on the trim, one day with his ladder right here at my window, his spattered desert boots on my eye level. I caught him giving me a glance through the trailing vines of ivy. Was he on the ESP channel to Alice? At her invitation he had his lunch with us on the deck. For my benefit, I think, he expressed the opinion that the planet was in for a new weather cycle. Nothing spectacular. Just drought and famine. The rising of the seas would come later. London, New York, Los Angeles, Tokyo, and Venice would experience a cleansing burial. How would those bells sound under water? He yawns after eating, tapping on his tummy like a gourd. He has a boyish uncouthness of manner, slouching down to sit on his spine, knees forward and spread, knobby head lolling, an elegant, somewhat simian manner of lifting his beer can by the top brim, sloshing the contents. Alice wears her dark glasses, avoiding the burn of his glance. It might have been a good time to bring up *A Hole in Space* but I had no idea what he might say. Almost anything he said, it seemed to me, would be in character.

Wednesday morning, just before nine, Dahlberg called. That caught me so unprepared I was almost eagerly friendly toward him. Harry had to drive to Plattsville, he said, which was more than forty miles due east, and made it impossible for Dahlberg to be traveling in the opposite direction. He was sorry. In my confusion I think I said we would miss him. When he hung up I found I rather regretted his departure from custom. Harry would not have done it. He would not have departed from principle. In Harry's view everything depended on the non-dependable state of affairs. I feared that it meant Dahlberg was feeling the pull of new contradictory attachments.

"I never expected him to call," I said to Alice.

She replied, "He's bringing me some real cider."

People have such exchanges all the time. We both appeared to be pleased. I waited till lunch to tell Alice I had some work at the library, so it was after two o'clock before I left the highway for Fork River.

It was not a good day. A high, gauzy cirrus diffused the light and increased the glare. We have days when no apparent wind to speak of will lean on the car. You get little response when you depress the gas pedal, as if you were climbing a grade. Some weeks back I read in the paper of these cars that proved to be *coasting* uphill. Somewhere in the Near East, I think. They were descending a grade, but when they let the cars coast they came to a stop, and then coasted upgrade. We all know the answer. An optical illusion. It looked upgrade because of the slopes and angles. It's amazing how irrational people are if you say, "Oh, that's an optical illusion." They feel better right away, although what you have told them is that they can't trust their eyes. When I have a similar disquieting experience I cast around for some rule of thumb to reassure me. The experience is unnerving, but the *rule* is reassuring. Things do not roll uphill. Any fool knows that. So when you see a car coasting uphill you're not at all disturbed, since you know it's downhill. Going up the slight incline toward Fork River I could see by the ditch weeds I had a strong tailwind, but the motor had a carbon ping, and was sluggish. Was there a problem? I reassured myself I had a tank of bad gas.

On the rim of the ravine, where the road suddenly dropped, did I imagine I heard a windborne surge of music, like that of a drifting radio signal? It blew away as the road lowered, as if it was part of an upper layer of air. It seemed to me there were fewer leaves on the cottonwoods but otherwise it looked the same as when I had last seen it. The willows looked less green in the diffuse light, and the shadows hardly cool enough to seek out.

I parked near the schoolhouse, the car crackling as it cooled. The customary pigeons were not clustered around the bell tower, or pacing up and down the ridge of the roof. There were no cawing crows or barking dogs. A village without people has a troubling stillness. Where was Mr. Lindner? I had assumed he had spotted my arrival, and would come out of the woodwork to discuss the weather. In which house did he live? Did *they* live? As I came in I had passed, on my left, a post with what was left of a box-like sign, about chest high. Looking back I could see the word ROOMS on a cracked piece of painted glass. If a lantern was put in the box at night, the sign would light up. I had all but forgotten that pre-motel period when local people took in tourists. The house that went with this sign, with a covered porch at the front, was boarded up on the first floor but had two dormer windows above the porch. One window stood open. Spread out to dry on the shingled roof of the porch were several undershirts, pairs of socks, and two pairs of Levi's, still so wet they looked black. I left the car, letting the door hang open, and walked around to the rear of the schoolhouse. The back door was ajar, propped open with a brick. Mounted on the inside of the door pane, like an ice card, was a sign that read

To Whom it May Concern
WELCOME
Back before dark.

I assumed the door had been left ajar to let out the heat. The building had a roof of sheet metal and glass, and would soon heat up. I opened the door to see Dahlberg, at the room's center, seated in the prescribed lotus position, his hands placed forward on his crossed legs, the palms up. He wore nothing at all, that I could see, but a film of perspiration. He looked like a heathen idol. On seeing me he closed his eyes.

"I'm sorry," I mumbled, thumped the door backing out, and heard him cry, "Kelcey, come back here!" I was not sure that I cared to. "Come back here!" he yelled. I let a moment pass, then I stepped in. He had several beer cans on the floor at his side: he patted the spot on the floor where I should sit. "Sit down," he said. I sat down. "You're not intruding, Kelcey. This is *your* project as much as it is *my* project. You like a beer?" I did not want a beer. We sat facing, high in the north gable, the glass panel showing the planet earth rising above the moon's horizon. Spellbinding! Prodigious! Stupefying! and ordinary. It would soon be on T-shirts with Brahms and Beethoven.

"Do you grasp it, Kelcey?" I liked the way he called me Kelcey. I felt it helped me to grasp it.

"It's the perspective," I said, prepared to go on. I knew quite a bit about perspective.

"No, no, no!" he groaned. That wasn't it at all. His head lolled forward on his chest as if suddenly heavy. It saddened me to have failed him. He had thought me smarter. Perhaps he had thought me smart enough to be included in. My heart pounded. I was ripe for the word, but it escaped me.

"Then what?" I asked, my mouth dry, but he had withdrawn into meditation. His eyes were closed. Here and there, like constellations, I detected buzzing clusters of insects. It's hard to get away from the world's fictions. Why couldn't I see what was there instead of what I'd read about it? High in the gable wasps droned at the mindless business of creation.

"Kelcey—"

"Yes?"

"You remember what He said?"

"Harry?"

Once more I had failed him. But he was quicker to recover.

"He said, It is finished. And it *was* finished. In two thousand years this is the first new beginning. It is the *earth* that is resurrected." I admired the way he had put it all together, nodding my head. "Love, hate, grand illusions, small illusions, you name it—"

I said, "Name what?"

152

"It's all been tried. Nothing works. If this doesn't work we'll have to write it off."

"The planet?" I asked.

"The planet."

"I think it might work," I said, "if what it takes is awe. It's the most awesome thing I've ever set eyes on—and failed to grasp."

"Kelcey, I've seen it on restaurant menus. The world in space. An old planet of the apes."

"What about yourself. You're a pretty reluctant prophet."

I regretted having said that. He looked chagrined, shamefaced. He moved his hands from his lap and saw, just as I did, that he was naked. "Harry's the true believer," I said. "He's got what it takes. And one thing it takes is no sense of humor. You're a very funny man."

He glanced at me, appreciatively. I just wish that Alice could have seen him.

"He's the believer," I went on, "you're his first disciple. You really make a first-rate space John the Baptist. I can go right along with you on that hole in space."

"You're kidding."

I shook my head. I was about to ask him if it *really* happened. What held me back? "It's sure beautiful from here," I gestured at the earth, floating in space, "but what do you propose to do when you get back?"

I could see that question alarmed him. Was I going too fast? "I've been giving some thought to it," I said, "and I wouldn't rule it out that I might be helpful. Besides the believers, you need the ones who just stay and wait."

My feeling was he was right on the edge of including me in. His head bowed, the vertebrae in his spine were prominent. Alice had remarked how scrubbed his scalp looked through the short pelt of hair. You get the same effect around the eyes of a short-haired cat. Dahlberg liked the heat, the oozing perspiration that relieved the soul's pollutions. I knew his manias. As a boy he had signed his name in blood.

"Look, Dahlberg, if anything should happen, somebody should be here to report on it. Who would know it? What will it be but another hole in the ground? I'm so close to the edge I no longer see the sunrise. It's the earth that turns. I see it curve out of the darkness into the sun's rays, like the globe on the Pathé news reels. You remember that? I've been a space bug ever since. That one whirled too fast for the better effects. Day and night are everlasting. It's the spinning globe that gives the wrong impression. Nor is it a mystery to me that we feel as we do at three o'clock in the morning. Look where we are! At the back rim of the night. What if the globe should stop spinning? I've given it some thought. Can you imagine what would happen when the word got around? No more sunrises? No sunsets. Just the light burning like a crack in a curtain at the rim of the world. But that's science fiction. Have you been to the mountains? You know how small things look on the plain? If you're up high enough, trains stop crawling. Higher yet, jets stop moving. Now if you just carry that to its conclusion, at some point in space time has stopped. It's all in suspension. My game is to zoom in from space on the Mesozoic period. Late research points out that the dinosaur was not just a big slug, but had strong family feelings, with what you might call stereo vision. He had to have something. Look how long he lasted. Another period I like is the dawn of man. Was it me Tarzan, you Jane, or less basic? I suppose the novelty was lost on them. Have you followed the latest rumor that he was a friendly, bow-and-arrow-type hunter? She was a hefty homebody and bone reader. They had a good life—while it lasted. Imagine looking out from that smoke-filled cave over ice fields in the winter, in the summer woolly mammoths wallowing in the swampy hollows. The moon anything you wanted to make of it. The caves appeal to me more than the grassy plains. For one thing, no place to hide. Why do the primates have this up ahead vision, with nothing behind? After all, there's more to be seen looking backward. You give up? Well, I'll tell you. It's less what they see than what they imagine. One thing leads to another, then an-

155

other, and they all lead to where we are. Who sees what is there? From here how empty it looks! A new beginning, right? Time for a landing party. If you had your pick, where would you choose? High in the Himalayas, or low in a primeval jungle? In the pure white Arctic, hunting for puppy seals, or right here in Fork River, no smog and no crowding. Good dentists, heart transplants, and air-cooled movies. Whatever you find on Mars you'll have to take it with you. In strictly practical terms this is the site for a landing. So why take off?"

I didn't want a casual, offhand answer. I could see he needed time to think it over. Who could explain, to a creative landing party, zooming in on what appeared to be a crisp mini-crater, that the armored thugs, battling like gladiators, were schoolboys at play on Saturday afternoon? A peace-type game, played during periods of cold war. How explain it to a spaceperson? "Well, I hope you know what you're doing," I said, "you *are* going to need a good navigator."

I didn't wait for his reply. It seemed cool outside, thanks to the film of perspiration inside my clothes. More leaves had fallen on the surface of the playground, and I was tempted to sweep them off. It seemed obvious, as Harry had pointed out, that the landing approach would be from up the river, gliding in as I had seen it done in the movies. On the top of the saucer a revolving blinker: the entrance through a trapdoor in the bottom. I found the space machinery convincing, but the prospect of the space-persons disturbing. Why these comic-strip Martians, with their repulsive hooded heads, fishy eyes, and dangling antennae? Why not invisible, the ultimate triumph! Just the stir of air, the irresistible attraction. I could see myself tempted. "Yes," I would say, "it came in like a top, with a purring vowel sound and an odor like crushed blossoms. Indescribably alluring, but not at all corny. I felt drawn myself. After all, what was there to lose but my clichés?"

Someone had closed the door to my car. On the windshield I found a penciled note on the back of a discount coffee coupon.

Not responsible for cars parked
near schoolhouse.
E. B. Lindner

Mr. Lindner was nowhere in sight. The clothes were still drying on the roof of the porch, and I noticed a small throng of birds, flocking. The winter in Fork River would be something to deal with. More of a sense of resignation, of abdication, but what a crystalline sky at the north chapel window, the earth swimming in the vibrant ether. Surely it would take less faith in the winter, but more body heat.

On the highway I was so absentminded I drove

past my turnoff, into Millard. They had strung a banner across the street advertising the days of the covered wagon. The men were growing beards. There would be a big parade on Halloween. Suddenly I felt the discomfort of a wireless set jammed with interference. What did these antics have to do with the view from space? What had led me to confuse the history of the planet with the history of man? Compared with his fellow creatures he was frivolous and fragmentary. He lacked history. Nothing human was alien to him, but who could say what was human? Until he had more history he was the missing link himself. I sat at the counter in what had once been a pool hall, but was currently a restaurant, dunking a cinnamon role into coffee under the observant eyes of the waitress. In her disapproving gaze I saw the look of the first visitor from space.

14

WIND WE HAVE all the time. It's the absence of wind,
or a slack in the wind we notice. One of my vivid
memories, as a boy, is that of a windless day. I
remember the puzzled, concerned glances people
gave the sky. On the plains the sky is where you look
for what seems to be missing, or when something
goes wrong. I looked up at it too, and saw one sky
going by overhead like paper blowing, and through
the gaps in it I saw another sky, with a rippled surface, pink as if the sun was rising or setting, and still
above that, strips of cloud thin as gauze blowing to
pieces right before my eyes. The wind that seemed
to be missing, on earth, was up there in the heavens,
blowing the sky around. I was old enough to grasp

that this was highly irregular. Later that evening we learned that three twisters had struck in Heber County, the town of Alston all but wiped off the map. That phrase strongly impressed me—a town wiped off the map. It makes sense in this country to speak like that, since the surface of the plain is map-like, the roads run straight east and west, or north and south, with sharp right angles at the intersections: from a few miles up it actually looks like a map, and the wonder is not that something blows away, but that it stays in place.

Last night, right out of the black, I woke up as if I'd heard a clap of thunder. The silence of the windless night made my ears ring. As if stirred by a bat's wing the curtain stirred at the window: a creak went through the house as if a weight pressed on it. Above the trees a diffuse phosphorescent glow made everything flat, with one dimension. Flat, rippling cirrus clouds drifted eastward. I had this wild fear that the air was departing. I took a breath and held it, as if it might be my last. And right at that instant a suck of air, as if in the wake of an invisible object, clawed up fistfuls of leaves and dust as if a helicopter was landing. Above the clouds screening the stars I seemed to hear a cosmic wind. Nights speak to us profoundly of what once happened, of what might happen in the presence of darkness. I gripped the sill but I felt no terror until I came back to bed and missed Alice. I chilled all over, as if I had been dipped in a deep freeze. My sensations were so primal I lacked a word for them. A plant might feel as much, or as little, as I did. There was not a shred of consciousness in it. I was in the world like a stalk of celery. Alice found me sitting up staring, as in a nightmare. She had been to the refrigerator: her breath smelled of low-fat milk. She says that I resisted her efforts to wake me although I was not asleep. I didn't want to give up, I didn't want to come back, from where I had been. In the morning I would say I had the damnedest dream—and it would be lost. I would not recover the sensation that must be common to everything but people. A purely sensuous being in the world. I lay back on the pillow and had this dream—is there a better word? In the yard below me two or three dozen little girls, in their birthday suits, stood in a circle like kewpies while the sprinkler wet them. At its center stood Alice, wreathed in veil-like clouds, poised like the Venus in Botticelli's Primavera, her head tilted so that the sprinkler water pelted her face. The children danced clockwise around her, shrilly piping some nursery rhyme. I gathered it must be a celebration, since they all looked so blithely happy. Water streamed down Alice's face, and clung to her skin like drops on a window. The scene was moonlit, or rather earth-lit, the glowing, cloud-wreathed planet filled half the sky, and was growing larger. Were we coming in for a landing? I remarked the absence of polar caps. Had they melted? The great globe of the earth was like a painted balloon. How beautiful it was! Out of a vast jade green sea only one peak jutted. The cleansing flood had come! I looked for Noah and his ark. I saw it all as clearly as the details on the globe in the Pathé news reels. We were coming in! As it all swept below me I realized there was no place to land. It was all one sea, the peaks had vanished, I saw fish leaping and birds flying, but in all of that vast sea no sign of man. I cried out something because Alice woke me, and switched on her light to have a close look at me. Seeing her troubled, puzzled expression I said, "Don't be surprised if people act crazy," as sober as a judge. It seemed to calm me, and in a moment I was asleep. I next remember waking to see Dahlberg and Alice at the foot of my bed, whispering to each other. His hands were green with paint, as if he had walked in from the woods.

Alice said, "Are you awake?"

I said that I was. I could be wrong, but I felt that Dahlberg almost looked at me with concern. God knows he's gangly, he's awkward, he has lumps on his neck, but there's something undeniably appealing about him. Something vulnerable, something expectant.

"You've been talking in your sleep something awful," said Alice "Who is Towper?"

"It might be Topler," said Dahlberg.

162

It pleased me to see them so anxious. With his green hands they made an interesting couple. "I know no Topler," I said, "but I once knew a Taubler."

"Who was he?"

"He was a genius," I replied. "He was crazy."

"You're running a fever," said Alice, and put her cool hand on my forehead, taking my pulse in a professional, nurse-like manner. "You've got to rest," she said, "you're overexcited."

I accepted that fact as obvious. Alice tilted the blinds to keep the light off my face, casting luminous reflections on the ceiling. Taubler would have loved it. He preferred the illusion to the reality. On the wall of his studio he had painted French doors that opened out on a view of the Mediterranean. At night the sky sparkled with stars he put on with the paint they used on watch dials. The moon was there, a green-cheese color, and the upper half of planet earth. If we studied it through his telescope it proved to be the upper half of a human skull. Art Tuchman thought he was a genius. It was all new to me. I didn't know what to think.

15

HAVE I SUPPRESSED IT? Was Taubler the space trip of my life? In the summer of 1939 I was a student in England, soaking up culture. All the talk about war led me to go to Paris for a two-week vacation while it was still there, and inhabited by Frenchmen. I arrived about daylight, in the Gare St. Lazare, and found it easier to walk than lose myself in the Metro. I saw that the secret of Paris was that the people who lived there lived everywhere: the air in the street smelled of all the rooms, kitchens, and closets being aired at once. I had been told about gay Paree: I didn't know what to make of its resigned sadness. Some people brushed against me, some made way for me, but none gave any sign of having seen me.

I towered above most of them. Little they seemed to care. A girl with teeth so black I thought they must be missing turned to give me directions, but not look at me. I had never experienced such indifference. I was amazed that a great teeming city could be so profoundly melancholy. No one had troubled to tell me. I had made this discovery all by myself.

Toward mid-morning I sat on a bench in the Luxembourg gardens, composing a postcard to my mother. I had seen Paris. I had not been too impressed by what I had seen. I found the gravel paths, the old women, the shrill-voiced children, more depressing than the small fry where I had come from. On the bench across the path, an older man—not elderly, but with his best years, as we say, behind him—sat slouched, his legs astraddle, his arms stretched along the back of the bench as if crucified. I thought him a handsome man, really, in a scholarly way, but down on his luck. The bottoms of his pants were not merely frayed, but so chewed at the back the cuff was missing. His right foot, turned on its side, showed the hole in both the shoe and the sock. His hands and the balding top of his head were tanned. This dozing old man symbolized for me what I had come to feel about Paris. A sadness bordering on dejection: a past with no prospect for the future, with another war rumbling on the horizon. I was touched and depressed by the impression that such a state of soul had become a way of life. I was about to leave when I noticed that he was not napping, but observing me through half-closed eyes. Was he thinking of asking me for money? Before he did I stood up to leave, but he signaled for me to remain seated. From his pocket he took a piece of white chalk and pretended to draw, on the air around me, the details of an invisible room. He put in the windows, the door, and hung pictures. On the bench at my side he added a figure. The large hat, with fruit or flowers, indicated that it must be a woman. Then he stooped and on the gravel path at my feet he signed the picture

H. TAUBLER

Unmistakable. Then he stepped back to look at what he had done. That habit of squinting through half-closed eyes seemed to be his custom. Did he like what he saw? He seemed to be of two minds. From the inside pocket of his coat, where it was fastened with a clip, he removed a sheet of paper, handed it to me. The page was ornamented with printer's devices, hands with pointing fingers, cat's eyes, capital letters, a clock without hands and the word OUI! OUI! OUI! in a row across the top and bottom. At the center of the page, in small type, I read

Don't be surprised if people act crazy.
Be surprised if they act human.

I looked up to see his hand extended toward me, palm up, so I gave him two French coins, and he thanked me. He was perfectly sober, he stood for some time with his fingers hooked in his vest pockets, then he strolled away on the frayed cuffs of his pants.

A day or two later, it might have been three, my time sense being affected, I was going along the wall of a cemetery when I saw the name H. TAUBLER. Was he a man who wrote his name on walls? A large piece of this wall had been peeled of its plaster, exposing the red bricks beneath. Along with the plaster part of a poster advertising an apéritif had disappeared. Was that his picture? He might think so, if he was crazy enough. Later that same day, on the Boulevard San Michel, I saw him scrounging in one of the big litter baskets for candy and cigarette wrappers. For the first time I noticed how, when he strolled along, he looked about the same from the front and the back. I didn't really know in which direction he was going until I moved in close.

I went to the Louvre, and on two occasions I went to a movie just to watch the newsreels, but most of the time I just wandered around, thinking I might stumble on Taubler. The light in Paris has a glow about it, as if full of blowing snow or sparkling dust. I found myself squinting most of the time, through half-closed eyes. I found the name H. TAUBLER on two of the pissoirs, signed to strips of torn posters, and early one evening, near the Gare Montparnasse, I was approached by a dirty book peddler. He had them under his arm. The one he showed me was a volume of Jules Verne, *Voyage to the Moon,* with tipped-in pornographic illustrations. The peddler was a hulking black-haired young man, wearing green-tinted motorcycle goggles. He looked more German than French. In French I said, "Not now. Perhaps another time," to indicate I was not the usual sort of tourist. It brought on a fit of wheezing laughter. He pushed up his glasses to wipe at his eyes. "Oh, Christ," he said in English, "that's a new one." He had a Brooklyn accent, a cheerful, blue-jowled smiling face. "You're American?" I asked him.

"Me?" he wheezed at me, "I'm Tuchman. Wait till he hears that one."

"He who?"

"You got to meet him. He won't believe it."

He took my arm and we walked up the street to the Metro stop on the Avenue du Maine. Three old men, seated on folding stools, were playing haunting, melancholy music. One of them was Taubler. He sat with a clarinet across his knees while the accordion player did an encore. When the music stopped I was introduced to him.

"What's your name?" Tuchman asked me. I told him. "Kelcey," he said, "this is Taubler. Taubler doesn't believe Americans are real. He thinks they're a hoax made up by the movies."

I could see that the idea pleased Taubler. He gripped the lapels of his coat in the manner of a public speaker, but he said nothing.

"Don't let me intrude," I said.

"He don't play," said Tuchman. "He's hard of hearing. But if he sits here with them people give them more money."

"Is he crazy?" I asked Tuchman.

Eight or ten people gathered around us to watch Tuchman laugh.

So this is what Paris is like, I said to myself. It was all new to me, and I liked having someone crazy to talk to. We stopped and had a *café noir* at a sidewalk café where Tuchman sold one of his books to a tourist. We all shook hands. At no time was I possessed by the feeling that I had come to Paris to be flabbergasted. It all seemed normal enough. It had simply never occurred to me that grown-up people, of their own free will, might actually choose to be peculiar, or that opinions might differ on what being peculiar was. Now that it had occurred to me it was not yet something I was prepared to admit.

That afternoon we went to see the newsreels together, where we saw the world preparing to go up in flames. Everybody was marching. We sat in the dark watching them march. Then we went to a Chinese restaurant on the Boule Mich which was up one flight, with tables at the windows. Right there below us an organ grinder was having an argument with his monkey. The monkey would throw his own hat on the ground, then stamp on it. Then they would change positions and each one would stamp on the other's hat. A large cluster of people formed a circle to watch them, blocking the walk. Taubler had the seat at the open window, framing the view. Using one of the bits of crayon he carried in his pocket—he needed different colors on different occasions—he printed H. TAUBLER on the sill of the window. It was new to me, but I did not let on that I found it unusual. When we got to the fortune cookies I had one that said I would make new friends and begin a new life.

In the days that followed I saw the name of Taubler all over Paris. Wall posters that were torn or defaced in some manner were his specialty. He did not modify or improve these exhibits: he appropriated them. He filled his pockets with select samples of litter he found in the gutters, or the trash bins. Anything that had served its own purpose was ready to serve his. He did not buy newspapers, but he would take the time to read everything posted at the news kiosks. He stood back, being farsighted, his hands firmly gripping the lapels of his jacket. I had the clear impression that an invisible person was holding him up. On the Friday of my last weekend I saw this blind man in front of the Gare Montparnasse with a telescope pointed at the clear blue sky. It was Taubler. He had put on a beret and a pair of blind man's black glasses. He looked scholarly. A sign fastened to the tripod said

EARTH VIEW
1 Franc

I dropped a coin into the cup that hung from Taubler's neck. In the eyepiece I saw my own lashes, but not much else. Then I made out the half shell of a walnut pasted to a piece of blue litmus paper. The seas were dry. It made a very convincing image of the shrinking globe. "How was it?" Taubler asked me.

"Shrinking!" I cried. I was beginning to get the hang of it. He folded up his telescope, took off his glasses, and we walked together up the Rue de la Gaieté. Along the way he bought a loaf of bread, a yard long, which he carried under his arm like an umbrella. We met Tuchman in the hall of the building we entered and walked up the stairs. I held the bread while Taubler went down the hall to use the water closet, then came back to unlock a door that was padlocked. It opened on an oblong room without windows, under a grime-dimmed skylight. On the back wall I could see a huge Paris Metro map, showing all the stops. At each stop the heads and arms of dozens of people sprouted like flowers, with the faces of red-cheeked, happy children. Faces also stuck up through cracks in the map, but not so happy. They clenched their teeth, or appeared to be howling. Here and there an arm thrust up, or a hand stretched out to grip something, hanging on for dear life. Tuchman beckoned me to come closer. At the Metro stop on the Boulevard Montparnasse one of the heads sticking up was mine. He caught my likeness. I had a brush cut hairdo and fuzzy cheeks. Until I stood in the room I didn't see the French doors in the south wall. They were framed by bright lemon yellow drapes, the green shutters thrown open on a view of the sea. The drapes were real, but the wine dark sea was a wall painting, with Taubler's name on it. The color was so brilliant I squinted at it, half closing my eyes. Drawn up to face the view was a real canvas beach chair, the floor around it strewn with the hulls of painted peanuts. They were so real birds would have pecked them. To the left of the doors, flush to the wall, was a planters seed box, the bottom covered with gravel. Out of this box grew a plant, or rather a beanstalk, the huge green leaves painted on the wall to where they grew through a hole in the ceiling. Two long strands of real rusted wire supported this plant against the wind, and held it upright. The light off the sea cast the pale leaf shadows along the wall. Turning back

172

to the view I saw a lopsided moon low in the sky. Peering closer I recognized planet earth and noted its resemblance to a human skull. There were cracks in it, or rather fissures, and on the bone-dry surface he had painted jewel-like cemeteries, the stones shining like gems. America appeared to have sunken, like a dead sea. A tiny white polar cap sat at the pole site, like a bandage. I turned aside to look at Tuchman, seated on a stool that had a high chair back painted on the wall. He leaned against it. "He's got his own system, Kelcey, and you'd better believe it."

I could believe it. Hadn't he already painted me into it?

"You can either work on the Metro or you can paste candy wrappers into dirty novels. We've got a new system going, but it still takes work."

"What would you say's the idea?" I asked him.

"You've got to make your own world, then live in it," said Tuchman. He was one of those big shaggy-dog types of people with the touch of something sweet and hopeless about him. I felt drawn to him. He had a pelt of black hair on his chest that made it hard for him to button his collar, gray eyes, and a big, soft Jewish mug. With Tuchman in it, Taubler's crazy system might work.

A week or so later, I've no idea, since we were living in our own time zone, Hitler and his pack invaded Poland and I was on a boat headed for the

States. I said I would write. Tuchman said he would write. Taubler, of course, said nothing. That was more than thirty years ago. All I've got to show for it is a copy of Zola's *Nana* illustrated with hand-torn candy wrappers, signed by H. Taubler. Wherever he is, I'm prepared to believe that his system works.

16

ALICE'S DR. FRIEDMAN will say my state of mind arises out of rather special circumstances. A fevered mind: a pattern of leisure: nights of lying awake rather than sleeping, and so forth. If an explanation is what you want, it is what you will get. On Monday I felt well enough to go with Alice over to her clinic. Nothing specific. A routine blood test. The elderly lady who took my blood seemed to see better if she removed her glasses. You know the routine. You extend the bare arm, the palm up, a remarkably vulnerable position. The rubber tourniquet is applied, the invisible vein is supposed to appear. Mine did not. She probed about for it. If I were picked up on the street I would be taken for a drug addict. She doubted aloud that I had veins, and an intern was called in to finish me off. He found my blood pressure high, and suggested rest. Might this be described as a special circumstance? On the way home we stopped for gas at Spivak's station, which gives Alice Blue Stamps, and I sat in the car while she did a little shopping. Spivak's boy, Ernie, had raised the hood to check the water and the oil. Through the gap between the hood and the cowl I could see his disembodied hands, working, the soiled fingers and bruised knuckles caked with grime, like belt pulleys, the nails blackened, the fingertips blunted, the back side of one finger glistening with nose drool, like a snail's track, the acid mantle of skin (I had been reading some offbeat medical papers) chapped along the seams, filmed over with oil impervious to water, groping with assurance for the dipstick, then, as if blind, for the battery water, a new kind of creature born out of the need millions of cars have to be serviced, a selective speeded-up evolutionary process, but when I blinked my eyes what I saw on the lids was beautiful beyond the telling of it, the planet earth, veined like marble, its torments stilled, its seas like glass, on which at that moment I sat in a trance observing myself observe. Is that so peculiar? Taubler would have signed it. Earth rising above the hood of a '72 Plymouth.

"You all right?" Alice asked me.

I could see that Alice thought I looked a little

strange. On reflection, it is my opinion that I should have spoken up. I frequently detected in Alice's gaze a willingness to share what I was thinking—even more than what I was thinking—but we both had our vested interests. Mine you know. The interests that weighed on me were hers.

Dahlberg had finished painting the trim and we had our last lunch together out on the deck. There was nothing more to paint. The front door was a possibility but Alice could not make up her mind about the color. Dahlberg smelled of the turpentine he had used to clean his hands and his brushes. He had that slightly peevish, boyish look that I knew Alice found so attractive. Alice loves to fuss with olives, celery stalks, radishes, bowls of nuts, and a variety of cheese dips, but she does not like to cook or open cans. This being the last day I also felt that his hostility had diminished. He was almost relaxed. He sat without cracking his knuckles or twisting his neck. We sipped vodka martinis, in chilled glasses, and nibbled at olives, celery stalks, bowls of nuts, a variety of cheese dips and stone ground wheat crackers. Dahlberg was very observant, but I wondered if he had noticed that Alice likes to fuss with food, rather than cook it. It often takes years to observe the obvious. In my own case, how long had it been that I had failed to notice Dahlberg's quick, lidded glances. Was it my pallor? I felt his concern. Alice seemed distant. Since she knows I dislike an open show of feelings, that is her way of admitting that she has them. For the first time I felt that I was part of the solution, rather than the problem. Was it my health? I felt a little queasy, but well enough. Would it surprise them if I said that it did not strike me as peculiar that two men shared the same woman? There was much to be said for it. My reluctance to say it stemmed from the fact that I didn't feel it with sufficient assurance. People in a moral dilemma who have lost their morals might feel very much as I did. I saw the dilemma clearly. I simply didn't feel the need to choose. If Alice or Dahlberg felt more strongly I would be the first to acknowledge their feelings. My queasy feeling stemmed from the fact that I often felt in abeyance. The man telling a story who interrupts it to say, "Where was I?"—that's very close to my problem. Somewhere between where was I, and where am I, is where I am. In a physical context I felt buoyant. Platforms that are built out over the water always give me a pleasurable apprehension. A loss of bearings. A giddy exhilaration. Some get that sensation with their second cocktail, but I could get it just by closing my eyes. In the blackness of space, under a lacquer of air, cloud-wreathed and condemned the planet floated, approaching the heart of the football season. Did Dahlberg grasp that? Was this the time to bring it up?

"We're going to pick up some plants at the nursery," said Alice. "The big ones in the cans. Dahlberg is going to help me."

The mention of the cans had reference to the time I cut my hand badly removing a plant. It required several stitches. That particular plant cost us about $90.00.

That was all right with me, and I sat on the deck enjoying the full bloom of my feelings. I wanted to keep the vibrations of that particular luncheon, and the concern for me that they were feeling. That I felt a shade of disquiet was part of it. In my opinion the truest measure we have of contentment is on a scale that registers discomfort, like these indoor-outdoor thermometers. On one you read how it is on the outside, the other on the in. I enjoyed the shifting pattern of leaf shadows on the lids of my eyes. I could hear the band playing at the neighborhood high school, the horns windblown in advance of the drums. What clever primate, pounding on a log, or blowing on his fingers, started what nothing would put an end to? Marching bands. Each member blowing his own horn, beating his own drum. In tune, in step, in a heaven of clatter. The pied piper a baton-twirling, high-stepping Venus. Everyone a performer! No one a copout! Or was I seeing things too clearly? Who can gaze without blinking at perfect human felicity? That is something you have to learn to live with in space, but I wondered about Alice. I meant to tell Dahlberg. In some respects I felt he was inexperienced with women. If you fall out of the habit of living with people their behavior can seem mighty peculiar. From space you can't take things one at a time. The stampede at the soccer match, the Miss America Pageant, and the oil slick off Santa Barbara are simultaneous events. You can't switch channels. It's all live, right around the clock. I dozed off, then I woke up with a start as a twisting gust of wind sucked the leaves upward. A top-lit moon, like a cone of lime ice, seemed to be tilted to dripping over Heber County. The night had the creamy pallor of snow falling in big butterfly flakes. What was it I heard? Dr. Friedman would tell me it was all in my ears. The cavemen had a gift for anticipation that was more than worrisome apprehension. Rainey identifies with early man, and seems to know. How those chaps would have guffawed, slapping their pelts, hearing us talk. Compared with those fellows our minds are loaded with shot, like a jumping frog's belly. Space traffic is quiet, comparatively speaking, but it seemed I could hear a few orbits creaking. Tedium with entropy? Had that troubled my sleep? How was I to explain to Miss Ingalls that all perception was extrasensory? It seemed obvious. The more extra the sensory, the more obvious. In the meantime, however, I lacked the gravity to consider what seriously concerned me. Where was my wife? Weightless in space her breasts would be bobbing. These are things that she may not have given much thought.

I got up to use the bathroom and found a note from Alice tipped in a corner of the mirror, the one place, everything considered, I'm inclined to look.

Kelcey darling:

Dahlberg says we can't be sure what this is, if it's not goodbye. In case Harry forgets, please have the light and power people turn off the lights. Also the phone. Who's going to need a phone? We're just not sure you really believe it. I've just got to. If he thought I didn't he'd do something reckless.

Love,
Alice

I could appreciate her choice of words, since she did not want to leave a message that might start a rumor. No matter how much a woman looks to the future she doesn't cut all of her ties with the past. The water and the lights would have been on her mind, spoiling her trip.

I7

ARE YOU SURPRISED to learn that the light and power people had no customers in Fork River? The last account, a Mrs. Overholtzer, had been closed in 1943. That's what the clerk told me but we had a very poor connection. I had the impression that other voices were trying to get through to me.

"I received and placed calls with a Mr. Harry Lorbeer," I said.

"Not over these lines," was her reply.

It seemed to me I heard a hum like space static. Could it have been Alice? When she hung up I heard no dial tone.

Over the weekend we had some gusty winds and heavy rains which made a shambles of Alice's new tomatoes, and kept me around the house. I find it hard to explain why I didn't miss her. Friends and lovers who make solemn pacts to meet in the beyond perhaps felt as I did. Less a loss than a period of waiting. It proved to be more disconcerting to do without Dahlberg, and the smell of the paint. Time and again I thought I heard the rattle of the ladders on Harry's van.

On Tuesday I drove over to Millard, and found the Fork River road gutted with a washout. The highway people had put up a roadblock, with blinkers. I left the car off the road and crossed the fields to the river, the west fork freshly clogged up with sludge and debris. Broken bottles and glass glittered in the shallows like strips of clear ice. I found two clapboards, one side smooth as if sanded, with pieces of yellow straw sticking through them like arrows. New to me, personally, but not unusual. At the heart of a twister many strange things happen. At a bend in the river, where silt had accumulated, I found a half-buried doorknob, like the egg of a seabird. Because the flooding had washed away a stretch of bank, I crossed over to follow the bed of the railroad. Weeds grew knee high between the rotting ties. The rails were crusty with rust, like corroding paint. I walked along with my head down to ignore a flock of hovering blackbirds, with yellow hatpin eyes. If I paused for a moment, they shrieked and dived at me. Nothing gives me the feeling of being in the wrong place, at the wrong time, like aggressive birds. They are in their element: I am out of mine. They lead me to wonder what my element is. Fish have the water, birds the air, but man wanders with his head down, and with good reason. I used up a little time throwing gravel at the birds. They swooped in on me from the rear, their wings stirring my hair, my head down between my hunched shoulders. The creature buried in my nature strained to surface: the skin tingled on my neck, cords pulled at my ears. A smarter animal than I have become would have turned back. Why is it that some places accommodate so easily to bizarre perspectives? Huge creatures once grazed here, tiny, dog-sized horses; saber-toothed tigers crouched on the rim rock. Red men speared their fish, white men set their traps, horse thieves, scoundrels, buffalo hunters looked up this ravine, screened by the willows, to the sanctuary of their imaginations. When I rounded the curve of the tracks up ahead, what would I find? The sun-cured, time-preserved, and suspended village, waiting for the return of the departed, or a ruined, shriveled ghost town given over to birds and vandals? Would I stand there, as we say, getting my bearings, wheeling slowly to look around me. Where was I? That is to say, in what element? Dahlberg would say that I had lost my nerve, but Alice knows my reluctance to see things too clearly. My talent's for waiting. I don't believe in rushing what is bound to happen. It wouldn't surprise me at all to feel the earth tremble, or note, on the sky over the canyon, the turbulence of air like ripples on water. The sense of buoyancy, of unearthly lightness, I had already felt and welcomed. The saucer-like object, gliding like a squid, tilted slightly as it zoomed in for a landing, would have lights around its rim like an electric eel, and give off a whirring sound like a musical top. On the veined lids of my eyes the whirling globe gathers into its vortex assorted flying objects, some identified. But I don't let it unnerve me like some people. You see, I don't believe in rushing what is bound to happen. Seeing planet earth, as I did this morning, rising on the chaste moon's horizon, I was seized with affection and longing for how things were in Fork River. I mean *really* were. Assuming, of course, there was such a place.